A
Harlequin
Romance

OTHER
Harlequin Romances
by ELIZABETH HUNTER

Many of these titles are available at your local bookseller,
or through the Harlequin Reader Service.

For a free catalogue listing all available Harlequin Romances,
send your name and address to:

HARLEQUIN READER SERVICE,
M.P.O. Box 707, Niagara Falls, N.Y. 14302
Canadian address: Stratford, Ontario, Canada.

or use order coupon at back of book.

THE SPANISH INHERITANCE

by

ELIZABETH HUNTER

HARLEQUIN BOOKS   TORONTO
WINNIPEG

Harlequin edition published September 1975

SBN 373-01912-2

Original hard cover edition published in 1975
by Mills & Boon Limited.

Copyright © Elizabeth Hunter 1975. All rights reserved.
Except for use in any review, the reproduction or utilization of this
work in whole or in part in any form by any electronic, mecha-
nical or other means, now known or hereafter invented, including
xerography, photocopying and recording, or in any information
storage or retrieval system, is forbidden without the permission
of the publisher.

*All the characters in this book have no existence outside the
imagination of the Author, and have no relation whatsoever to
anyone bearing the same name or names. They are not even
distantly inspired by any individual known or unknown to the
Author, and all the incidents are pure invention*

The Harlequin trade mark, consisting of the word
HARLEQUIN and the portrayal of a Harlequin, is registered
in the United States Patent Office and in the Canada Trade
Marks Office.

Printed in Canada

1912

CHAPTER ONE

RACHEL ANDREWS made a last effort to damp down the indignation that burned ever more brightly as she surveyed the man opposite her. It didn't help that she had brought his visitation on herself by appealing to her stepmother's family to help with the upbringing of her young half-sister.

'I don't wish Rosita to go to Spain!' she said out loud.

Señor Jerónimo Parades Lucot had the temerity to look amused. 'Rosita has certain responsibilities in Spain. Carmen was the heiress to much property and now that she is dead it will naturally devolve on her daughter. It was understandable that Carmen should live in England – her husband was an Englishman – but Rosita must learn to take her place in Spanish society and take an interest in the lands that will one day be hers.'

It all sounded so reasonable, but it didn't stop the cold hand of fear clutching at Rachel's stomach. Rosita had given her a reason for making plans for them both, for finding herself a job to keep them, even for the rather tatty couple of rooms that had been the best she could afford to house them. What would she do all alone, with no one to call her own?

She swallowed hard, allowing her temper to rescue her from the bleak picture of the future she had painted for herself. 'I know Carmen was your cousin,' she began, 'but that doesn't give you the right—'

'I have every right to look after your sister.'

'My father made me her legal guardian!' Rachel protested.

'Your father died first,' Señor Parades retorted. 'Carmen made somewhat different arrangements for the care of her daughter. I have a copy of her will with me, but I think you would not be much wiser if I gave it to you to read. It's enough for you to know that Rosita is now the responsibility of the Parades family.'

'And that means you?' Rachel burst out bitterly.

He inclined his head, his dark eyes glinting across the table at her. 'That means me as the head of the family,' he concurred.

Rachel slumped in her chair. 'I wish I'd never written to you! I should have left things as they were! We were happy, Rosita and I—'

'I should have found out sooner or later,' he cut her off. 'One cannot keep such things a secret for ever. And Rosita would not have thanked you, Miss Andrews. I think this—' he looked expressively round the shabby room – 'is not what either of you are accustomed to?'

Tears stung Rachel's eyes. 'My father—' she broke off, unable to continue. She was afraid that he already knew all about her father and had dismissed him as being everything that he despised. Her father had been a weak, affable man whose acquaintance with worldly success had not even been on nodding terms, yet he had married two devastatingly beautiful women and he had made them both happy in his way. Her own mother she could scarcely remember, but Carmen, lovely, indolent, and very Spanish, had taken her predecessor's child to her heart and had more than made up for any lack that Rachel might have known. It was only now that Carmen was dead that Rachel had been forced to come to terms with the fact that Carmen had not been *her* mother, that she had no Spanish blood in her veins, but was suddenly an outsider cut off from the only bit of her family that was left to her.

She looked up and saw that the Spaniard had been watching her closely. She felt quite suffocated by the dislike she felt for him. He was taller than most of the people she knew and very, very sure of himself. His eyes and hair were as dark as Carmen's had been and he shared her olive skin. The family resemblance between them was very strong, but it

6

did nothing to endear him to her. Where Carmen had been loving, if only because she had never had the energy to apply herself to disliking anyone, her cousin was coldly indifferent. He had a cruel twist to his mouth and the ability to hide his thoughts behind his naturally arrogant expression.

'So,' he said, 'we are agreed, Miss Andrews, are we not? Rosita will be cared for by my mother, where I can keep an eye on her and teach her what she will need to know about her future responsibilies.'

Rachel glumly nodded her head. 'I suppose so. But I shall consult a solicitor before I finally hand her over to you, *señor*. My father's wishes for his daughter must count for something, surely?'

'Indeed,' the Spaniard agreed. 'I have made inquiries as to what are the best arrangements that can be made to meet with his wishes for you both. Rosita's future we have dealt with.' He smiled suddenly, revealing strong white teeth. Caught unawares by this unexpected display of friendliness, Rachel felt winded. In other circumstances, she reflected uneasily, she would have found him dangerously attractive. He had an aura of masculine strength that her father's different charm had given no weapons to cope with. If anything she was more afraid of Señor Parades than she had been before.

She looked down at her hands, avoiding the amused appreciation in his eyes as he looked her over in a way that she thought indecent on such a short acquaintance. She lifted her head.

'I suppose you know that Rosita can't speak more than a few words of Spanish?' she challenged him.

He shrugged his shoulders. 'It matters little. In Spain, many of the aristocracy speak English in their homes. When she wishes to make herself understood by anyone else, she will soon learn how to express herself.'

'You don't care if she's lonely and – and miserable, do you?'

'It is no good arguing with me any more, Raquel. Rosita is my responsibility, not yours. You will accept that I am right in this matter, no? Come, *hija*, things will go much more easily when you make up your mind to leave everything to me. The burden of your sister's future is too great for a young girl like you to carry. It is not to be thought of!'

Her eyes flashed. 'I suppose you think you'll do better simply because you're a man—'

His laughter was gay and contagious. The colour rushed into Rachel's face as her anger died away to be replaced by an embarrassed awareness of his admiring amusement. Why, he didn't see her as a person to be taken seriously at all! To him, she was just a pretty face and he thought so little of her that he didn't even bother to hide his enjoyment of the encounter.

'I have other advantages,' he told her.

'Not in my book! Women don't have to sit at home and obey orders any longer, not in this country!'

'Did they ever?' he inquired.

Rachel was not prepared to argue the point. 'I don't know,' she admitted. 'The point is Rosita is more English than Spanish and she ought to be allowed to stay in England with me!'

His eyes met hers and held them very much against her will. 'It is strange that you should speak Spanish well when Rosita has only a few words,' he remarked.

'Car–Carmen preferred to use her native tongue round the house,' Rachel explained.

'Yet Rosita never learned enough to please her mother in this way?'

Rachel's cheeks burned. 'Rosita was younger – still at school, and she didn't have much time—'

Señor Parades sighed heavily. 'And she is as lazy as Carmen used to be?' he suggested.

'Yes,' Rachel admitted.

He sat back in his chair, his expression inviting her to join

8

in his amusement. 'If she wants to find out what the young men are saying to her when they pass her on the street, she will learn very quickly! I imagine she is like her mother in that too?'

Rachel repressed a smile with difficulty. Carmen, whose views on family life were above reproach and very firmly held, had dearly loved to flirt when the occasion had presented itself to her and there was no doubt that Rosita was already well able to put boys far older than herself in a whirl. She was seldom without half a dozen strong young men all falling over themselves to do her bidding.

'She has a way with the opposite sex,' Rachel admitted.

Señor Parades glanced sharply at her. 'You have not been able to control her?' he accused.

There was no answer to that. 'She means no harm,' Rachel defended her sister. 'I d-don't disapprove – not really! I expect I'd like to be able to do it too. Rosita always says I'm jealous of her!' Now whatever had made her tell him that? She stole a quick look at him and was relieved to see that he was not even looking at her. 'I'm seven years older than Rosita,' she hurried on, 'and I had – had other interests when I was seventeen other than boys—'

He was looking at her now all right! The muscle at the side of his mouth quirked, but otherwise he was as serious as she. 'I am glad I did not know you in those days,' he said.

'I haven't changed so much!' she shot at him.

'If you say not,' he agreed amiably. 'A certain reticence is charming, but it should not be taken too far.' He considered the point, his eyes gleaming at her. 'I think you do yourself an injustice, Raquel. What you lack is confidence, not interest. He will be a lucky man who supplies that lack. With your intelligence and spirit it should make a very interesting mixture.'

Rachel glowered at him. 'So is dynamite,' she pointed out.

'In the wrong hands, but when it is controlled by the right

person—' He left the sentence in the air to be completed by her own imagination.

Rachel cleared her throat. 'We were talking about Rosita,' she reminded him carefully.

'No, no, we had *finished* talking about Rosita,' he answered. 'We had just come to the point when I was about to tell you what I have arranged for your own future.'

'*My* future?'

'But of course. Did you think I would leave you to struggle on here by yourself? Your need to be cared for is as great as, if not greater than, your sister's.'

'I've managed up to now!' she said, stung.

'You have done your best, but I cannot approve that you should continue like this. These rooms are not for you! Neither do I like to think of Rosita's sister serving drinks to men in a bar!' He silenced her with a gesture. 'Please do not interrupt. Your salary as a secretary was not enough to support you both and so you took this other job to help out. Very admirable, but *not* what your father would have wished for you, or Carmen either!'

'I had no choice!' Rachel protested frantically. 'It's six months since – since it happened. One can't live on fresh air!'

'You should have written to me sooner,' he rasped. 'Why didn't you?'

'Rosita—'

'Rosita is a child. You are an adult, Miss Andrews!'

But Rachel hadn't felt much like one, she remembered, when the news had been brought to her that her parents had been in a car crash, that her father was dead and her stepmother in a coma from which she was unlikely to recover. She had never found out why Carmen had been driving that day, in a thick fog, when she was usually far too indolent to take the wheel unless pressed beyond endurance. Nor had Rachel ever discovered why they had gone off the main road, towards the sea, returning to the overcrowded route a little further on. That Carmen should have come out of an unmade road with a more or less concealed entrance, without glancing either to left or right, had been more than probable, but it had not helped much to know her stepmother to be in the wrong, when Rachel had dashed down from London on the first available train and had arrived barely in time to see her lovely, unmarked face, apparently sleeping, before she too had died, having survived her husband by only a few hours.

Rachel, at her wits' end to know how she was going to cope with her father's debts, let alone the double funeral and everything else, had been less than patient with Rosita. 'You'd better come back to London with me,' was all she had said.

'Never!' Rosita had affirmed.

But in the end she had had to. Rachel had moved out of the room she had had to herself for the last two years and had found this attic further out in the suburbs. It was cheaper than the room, but Rosita was an expensive young person to have around and Rachel had soon found that they simply could not manage on what she was being paid. So she had taken the second job as a barmaid at a nearby pub in the evenings to help to make ends meet. The greatest disadvantage had been that she had been working almost every waking hour and had no time to spend with her erratic young sister at all. When she had found out that Rosita had been entertaining some rather slippery young men alone in the attic in the evenings, Rachel had written to Carmen's family seeking financial help. It had been a blow to her pride, but she had done it, despite Rosita's sulks and her own feeling of failure, not only on her own behalf but also on her father's, because the Andrews should have managed on their own, without crying for help to strangers – strangers who were also foreigners and who had always looked down on Carmen's English husband, seldom writing to and never visiting Carmen or any of her family.

'I didn't think you'd want to know,' she said to Señor Parades, who was still waiting for an answer.

He looked shocked. 'Carmen was my cousin, why should I not want to know?'

'You didn't when she was alive!'

'On the contrary, I watched over her interests very closely. Several times I tried to discuss her inheritance with your father, but for some reason he refused to take an interest in her estates. At first, Carmen refused to take any interest also, saying it was for her husband to look after all such matters, but at last she was brought to see that things could not go on that way. She told me I was to do as I thought best on her behalf and I have looked after her property ever since.'

'Even so,' said Rachel huskily, 'that may give you some rights in a say over Rosita's future, but it doesn't give you any rights over me! Take Rosita to Spain if you must, but I shall stay here. I like my job and I like living in London!'

He looked stern. 'If you cannot speak the truth it would be better if you said nothing,' he chided her. 'I have made inquiries into your job and I am satisfied that it will never lead to a great career for you, so you need not tell more lies trying to make me believe that your life will be blighted for ever if you do not go on there. I have already told them you are leaving and that you will forgo a week's salary in lieu of notice. I sent them my cheque for that amount before coming here.' He smiled faintly. 'It seems to me that you worked very hard for not much reward,' he added.

Humiliated that he should know exactly what she had earned, Rachel was quick to contradict him. 'Secretaries are very well paid! They're very much in demand!'

'Is that why you became one?'

She shook her head. 'I wanted to go to university, but it came at a bad time for my father and so I took a secretarial course instead. I thought if I still wanted to I could become a mature student later on.'

'Much later on!' he teased her.

'I'm twenty-four!' she burst out.

His half-shut eyes took in every detail of her tow–headed blondeness, her fine grey eyes, and the wide, mobile mouth that was made for laughter and strong emotion and was at perpetual war with her straight, sensible nose and a small, stubborn chin. She was not pretty in the accepted sense, but she had the kind of face that was easy to look at and a complexion that outclassed any other he had ever seen.

'So?' he said.

'So you can't make me do anything! You can't give in my notice for me and tell me what to do! It's a good thing you haven't taken my home away from me too, because you'd find it a lot more difficult to talk my landlord into letting me stay on here than you will in persuading my employer to give me my job back – and I insist that you do that right away!'

'But, Raquel—'

'My name is Rachel, not Raquel!'

He smiled openly at her. 'I prefer Raquel.'

She stirred uncomfortably. 'What has that got to do with it?'

He made an expressive gesture with his hands that somehow summed up his attitude to all women, both the pretty ones and their plainer sisters. 'Raquel suits you better, it has more allure than the English Rachel.'

She stared at him, her heart beating painfully against her ribs. With difficulty she forced her attention back to the matter in hand. 'I *need* my job!' she said in a low, timid voice. 'You must see that, *señor*. You *must!* I have to earn my own living and stand on my own feet. You may be related to Rosita, but you're not related to me! It would be much easier if we both remembered that – don't you think?'

It was obvious that he did not. 'What peculiar ideas you

have!' he marvelled. 'My cousin was married to your father, isn't that enough for you? What sort of family would we be to allow you to live alone and support yourself when there is no need for you to do either? No, no, it is all decided, *pequeña*. You will come to Spain with your sister and my mother and Abuela will look after you both!'

'But your mother isn't *my* aunt, and Abuela isn't *my* grandmother—'

His eyes glinted with laughter. 'I defy you to persuade Abuelita that you are not her granddaughter!' he challenged her. 'In Spain we like to have large families with the most complicated relationships. What difference is there in being a granddaughter, or a step-granddaughter? It is all the same!'

'Except that Rosita has an inheritance to go to! I don't fancy being the object of your charity!'

'That is something which you will never say again!' he told her, his voice hard and implacable. 'If you think it, no one can stop you from doing that, but you will not insult my family by voicing such sentiments aloud. Is it understood?'

Rachel made one last attempt to make him change his mind. 'I can't see that my wanting to be independent is insulting your family. You see, we don't even think the same way! It would be disastrous!'

He was silent for a long moment and when he spoke again his voice was soothing and, she thought, abominably patronizing. 'Yet you have always wanted to visit Spain, Raquel. Who was it who always begged for more stories of Carmen's relations and the things she did as a child? It was not Rosita, but you, was it not? You are not much older than your sister – far too young to be left to your own devices in London without the first idea of how to protect yourself against unwanted suitors and the like! No, *cara*, you will come to Spain and be properly chaperoned, setting a good example to Rosita, who will undoubtedly find our ways very strange

14

at first.' His face relaxed into a teasing smile. 'Besides, too much rebellion in a woman is not agreeable to any man, as Carmen would have been the first to tell you. I've enjoyed doing battle with you, but it's time now for you to give in and admit that my way is best for you both and we will hear no more about your lack of fortune and having to make your own way in the world! You are a young girl, *niña*, not a man that you have to worry your head about such things!'

'Thank you very much!' she retorted. 'But the Andrews have their pride too and—'

'*Basta!*' he cut her off. 'That is enough!'

Rachel sat up very straight. 'I haven't begun!' she assured him. 'You've had your say and I don't agree with anything you've said! I'll do as I like! I'll—' She cast her eyes round the room, seeking inspiration, and came to his face, a peculiar sensation of panic rising within her as she met his eyes and knew that she was going to lose this particular battle and that she'd go meekly off to Spain at his behest and that *that was what she wanted to do*!

The amused smile in his eyes told her that he knew he had won too – more, that he had never expected anything else, and her face burned with humiliation that he should have read her so accurately. Supposing he knew about the delicious feeling of relief that had engulfed her, and how eagerly she wanted to see the place where Carmen had been born and had been brought up? If he did, she would never be able to gainsay him again with the smallest hope of bringing off a victory, and that was not to be thought of!

'*Señor*—'

'As I am your cousin it would be quite proper for you to call me Jerónimo,' he interrupted her.

She showed her teeth, unable to completely hide her smile. 'Jeremy?' she suggested. After all, if he preferred the Spanish version of her name, why shouldn't she retaliate by calling him by the English version of his?

'If you like,' he said agreeably.

The joy went out of her small rebellion. She didn't think that Jeremy suited him at all. He was far too arrogant and masculine for any normal name! Besides, she thought Jerónimo was much more attractive than its English version, with the 'J' pronounced as an 'H' in the Spanish way. Jerónimo was the name of heroes! There had been the Red Indian chief who had been given that name and whose courage had lingered on in the American memory to such an extent that their crack troops still called on his name when they parachuted into enemy country. This Jerónimo looked a bit like a Red Indian too, she thought, and he behaved like one as well, ruling the women of his family as if they were of no more account than the squaws of his namesake.

'Will I be able to get a job in Spain?' she asked in a small voice.

He shrugged his shoulders. 'Eventually. I have one in mind for you that you may like, as a matter of fact, but it's too soon to speak of that just now. You will have enough to do settling Rosita into her new surroundings. She will need you until she has grown used to our Spanish ways.'

There wasn't a word about the possibility of Rachel feeling homesick, or feeling strange in a foreign land, and *she* hadn't a drop of Spanish blood in her veins!

'What makes you think that I'll be able to help her?' she demanded indignantly, but he only laughed, reaching out across the table and clasping her hands in his in a grip that made her gasp.

'You'll take to Spain like a duck to water!' he assured her, much amused. 'And Spain will take to you. With those silver looks of yours, my mother will have to watch you like a lynx and, if you escape her watchful eye, you will have me to answer to, *mi bellisima* Raquel, and you will find me very strict. There will be no more of this barmaid nonsense, or anything like that!' He turned her hands over in his and examined her palms and nails, ignoring her attempt to pull them out of his grasp. 'You have a long lifeline,' he told her.

'Shall I tell you what your future will be?'

'Can you read hands?' she asked him, feeling rather shattered.

'A little. I can tell you that you will like the change in your circumstances very much. You will be very happy in Spain. You will marry a Spaniard and you will have many children—'

'I suppose he will be tall, dark and handsome?' Rachel scoffed.

He shook his head. 'I don't know. You will have to visit the *gitanas* if you want to know that sort of thing.'

She stared down at her hands, struggling to suppress the sharp disappointment she felt as he released her wrists and turned away from her. She had wanted to be told that her future husband would be as tall and as dark as Jerónimo Parades Lucot!

'The gypsies will tell one anything!' she said.

His mocking smile recalled her to reality. 'If you believe hard enough you will get what you want, but you have to believe in your own fate!'

That was the trouble, she thought; she didn't believe in herself enough for that and, as she couldn't possibly want what she had thought for one mad moment would be unbelievable happiness, it was probably just as well.

'I don't think you know what you're talking about,' she muttered.

He ran a finger down her straight, sensible nose and grinned. 'Oh yes, I do! Is that noise Rosita coming in? Does she always slam the door like that? My mother will not approve if she does!' He bent a little closer and Rachel could feel his warm breath on her lips. 'Shall I tell her, or will you, that you are coming to Spain with me?'

'I think I'd better,' Rachel whispered. 'I'll tell her about the glories of Granada and—'

But she never had the chance to say what else she would tell Rosita about, for her sister burst into the room, looking more like a full-blown rose than the rosebud her name implied, her eyes sparkling with remembered pleasure, her lipstick smudged, and her hair roughed up in a careless way that brought a frown to her cousin's eyes.

'Rosita!' Rachel mouthed at her.

But her sister was beyond anything that Rachel could say to her. 'It was marvellous!' she breathed, 'simply marvellous! You should have come, Rachel darling, instead of sticking at home as always!' Her eyes took in her cousin's tall frame silhouetted against the window and her eyebrows rose dramatically. 'Was *he* why you didn't come? How sly you are!'

'Rosita!' Jerónimo's voice was like the crack of a whip. 'That will be enough. Come here where I can see you better, and kindly explain where you have been to come home in such a state!'

To Rachel's astonishment, her sister crossed the room without a murmur. She looked up at her cousin, her eyelashes drooping against the soft curve of her cheek.

'You have a Spanish accent,' she told him in the husky tones she reserved for getting her own way with the men of her acquaintance. 'You must be one of Mother's relations. Which one?' She opened her eyes wide to give him the full benefit of her liquid brown eyes. 'Apart from being the handsome one,' she added on a would-be uncertain note.

'I am your cousin Jerónimo,' he answered abruptly. He put out a hand and ran it through Rosita's already chaotic hair. 'You had better not behave like a baggage when you're in Spain or you will make yourself very unpopular! I take it you have been out with some young man?'

'Young *men*,' Rosita corrected him gravely. 'Rachel doesn't approve of them singly—'

Jerónimo threw back his head and laughed. 'Much you care what Rachel thinks, young woman! I'll bet you've been leading her a mad dance! Don't try it with me, *carita*, or I'll make you sorry you were born!' He bent his head and kissed

18

first one cheek and then the other. 'Oh, Rosita, how very like your mother you are!'

Rosita preened herself, delighted with her new cousin. 'Tell me more about how I must behave in Spain? I shall like to go to Spain with you! It'll make a change from having Rachel disapproving of me all the time!'

'Very well.' He seemed pleased by the request. 'Go and tidy yourself and then I'll tell you all about it.'

She smiled up at him. 'Are we going soon?' she prompted him.

'At the end of the week, if Rachel can be ready by then. You will have to help her pack your things and decide what you want to bring with you.'

Rosita pouted sulkily, casting Rachel a look of open dislike. 'Why does she have to come? *She*'s not related to you!'

Jerónimo stiffened. 'Carmen would have wished it. Please go and tidy yourself at once, Rosita!'

Rachel would have gone with her sister, but Jerónimo's hand restrained her. 'Where has she been? Do you know?'

Rachel swallowed. 'I think she did tell me,' she said, knowing that Rosita had done nothing of the sort. 'She – she – I don't suppose it was nearly as bad as it looked!'

'It was every bit as "bad as it looked", and you don't even know whom she was with! It's just as well you're both coming to Spain if that's your idea of being responsible for Carmen's daughter!'

Rachel blinked, horribly aware how near she was to tears. 'I did my best. I can't make Rosita tell me things she doesn't want me to know. She probably came in like that deliberately—'

His fingers bit into her arm. 'Rosita,' he said slowly and with brutal clarity, 'is completely beyond your control and you are not even shocked by her behaviour, so presumably you can see nothing wrong in her playing around with these unknown young men! You'd do the same if you had the opportunity, wouldn't you? Well, for once you have the opportunity, Raquel Andrews, and *this* is why you're coming with me to Spain!'

He pulled her roughly against him and touched his lips to her own. Rachel uttered a wild sob and pulled away from him, but she was not fast enough. His arms swept round her, holding her closer still, and he kissed her with a fierce urgency that turned into ecstasy against her lips.

When he released her she was shaking. It was temper, she told herself, but if this were anger she had never experienced its like before. *'How dare you?'* she said in broken tones. 'I certainly shan't go to Spain with you now!'

He was not at all repentant. On the contrary, he was smiling. He fingered her hair, pushing it back from her face. 'Of course you are coming,' he growled at her. 'You are coming because I say so — and my mother will chaperon you both, and you will be very good, no?'

'I don't know,' she said.

He stroked the line of her cheek, drawing the ready colour up into her face. 'It will please me very much to have you in Spain, little cousin, and so you'll come?'

Rachel took a deep breath. 'Yes,' she said.

CHAPTER TWO

ROSITA seemed intent on making everything as difficult as possible. She could see no reason for her sister accompanying her to Spain and she said so loud and long.

'How did you persuade him that you had to come too?' she asked Rachel for the umpteenth time.

Rachel looked up from the suitcase she was packing. 'He didn't give me any choice.'

Her sister made a face at her and Rachel could feel her own temper flaring within her. 'Why do you want to go on your own?' she added, a slight edge to her voice.

Rosita shrugged. 'They're my family, not yours!'

'I'm well aware of that!' Rachel snapped.

'Jerónimo is *my* cousin!'

Rachel stood up, exasperated. 'You're welcome to him! If you want to know what I think of him, I shall be only too glad to tell you. I think he's arrogant and far too sure of himself! I can't think of anyone I dislike more than *your* cousin and, if he's a sample of *your* family, you're more than welcome to the lot of them!' She slammed the suitcase shut and strode across the room towards the door to find herself face to face with Jerónimo coming in. 'And that's another thing!' she stormed, addressing him directly. 'Who gave you permission to have a key to *my* front door? It's intolerable never knowing when you're suddenly going to appear!'

His eyebrows rose. 'If you guarded your tongue better you wouldn't find yourself disconcerted so often!' he retorted. 'Are you packed yet?'

'I am!' Rosita claimed virtuously.

'Not quite,' Rachel admitted. What time had she had? She had only that minute finished folding the last of Rosita's clothes and putting them in her suitcase.

'Then please finish now. Rosita and I will amuse ourselves while you do so. I have something to say to her anyway and this is as good a time as any.' He held the door open for her, the glint in his eyes daring Rachel to utter the words that were choking her. He shut the door firmly behind her, shutting her out of not only the room, but from the family discussion within. For two pins Rachel would have thrown it open again, to ram home the point that until they had actually shut the front door for the last time to go to the airport, this was *her* flat and he was no more than a guest partaking of *her* hospitality. But she hadn't quite got the courage to do any such thing. Let them have their family secrets, she thought. Why should she care?

It had been a long, hard week. Her ex-employer had been frankly curious about her future and she had been touched by what she had thought was a genuine concern for her.

'You do know what you're doing, Rachel?' he had said to her. 'That young man isn't the kind to be easily managed by any woman. He's kind of young to be your mother's cousin, isn't he? I shouldn't like you to get yourself into trouble, my dear. He may be very attractive, but what do you know about him?'

Rachel had told him that she was merely escorting Rosita to Spain, to the bosom of her family, and that she herself might well return after that. Her employer's brow had cleared. 'You'll always be welcome here,' he had assured her. 'I don't mind telling you that I was quite put out when Señor What's-his-name told me he would be looking after you from now on. I'd always thought you such a sensible girl!'

'You didn't like him?' Rachel had accused, sensing an ally.

Her employer had laughed. 'Yes, I liked him,' he had answered. 'But I was afraid *you* liked him a great deal too well! Understandable if you had! He had a shattering effect on the distaff side of the office. Any one of them would have gone off with him if he had so much as crooked his little finger! And yet the men didn't dislike him either. If you haven't fallen for him, I expect he'll look after you very well and give you a good holiday. The Spanish have a great deal of family feeling, or so I've always understood.'

Rachel had gone home feeling quite friendly for once towards Señor Jerónimo Parades Lucot. She had even admitted to herself that it wasn't only the girls in the office who had found him attractive. Her own heartbeat quickened every time she saw him, and that had been quite a lot. He had been in and out of her flat, organizing their last few days in England with a ruthless efficiency that had brooked no argument from either sister. Rachel, though she would have died sooner than have admitted it, had found it rather pleasant to be told what to do and when to do it, and not have those hundred and one worries that had plagued her over the last few months. If she was not grateful to him for any other reason, she was grateful for that.

Her friendly feelings had not lasted long. Jerónimo had met her at the door, a smug and rather triumphant Rosita hanging on his arm.

'Where have you been?' he had demanded in such a high-handed manner that she had stood stock still in the doorway and stared at him.

'Out!' she had said in a high, cool voice.

'For three hours? And without telling anyone where you were going?'

'I didn't know I was being timed!'

His hand had closed over her shoulder, forcibly propelling her inside the flat and closing the front door behind her. 'Well, now you know better! What did you expect, Raquel? That no one would worry when you were gone for so long – and without a word to Rosita as to when she might expect you back?'

'She's never worried before!' Rachel had observed dryly.

'Perhaps she hasn't told you when she was worried!' he

had snapped back. 'This independence must cease, Raquel! My mother has enough to do without having to spend her time seeking for you whenever you think you will take yourself out—'

'What I do is my own business!' she had cut him off.

He had shaken his head at her. 'Are the English so lacking in manners that they cannot conform to any restraint? Did you never tell Carmen where you were going and what time you expected to be back?'

'I suppose so,' Rachel had admitted reluctantly.

Jerónimo had shrugged his broad shoulders. 'Then you will treat my mother to the same respect. It is understood?'

Disheartened, she had nodded, bitterly aware of Rosita's enjoyment of the whole incident. There had not been much friendliness between herself and Jerónimo after that. She answered only when he spoke to her directly and then as seldom as possible, but when he came upon her unexpectedly, her resolution faltered in the most ridiculous way and she would hate herself for finding him so attractive. It was as if there was some invisible cord he held in his hand and could jerk at will, undermining her defences against him. Handsome is as handsome does, she reminded herself dourly again and again, but with less and less conviction, for it wasn't what he *did* that made the prickles run up and down her spine whenever he looked at her with that intimate gleam of laughter in the back of his eyes. Indeed, she only hoped he couldn't read her mind as easily as he had on one or two other occasions – like the time he had told her she should take with her the battered teddy-bear that had been her own mother's last present to her. 'Put it in your suitcase,' he had said. 'You'll only be lonely for each other if you don't!'

She felt for it now at the bottom of her suitcase, touching the familiar bald patches with gentle fingers. Perhaps, she thought, Rosita was more Spanish than she had ever supposed. She could certainly manage Jerónimo better than Rachel could ever hope to do. It wasn't Rosita who was continually running up against the rough side of his tongue. On the contrary, Rosita had been as good as gold, doing her share of the housework and looking as though she had *always* done it, and making no attempt to run wild with her friends in the usual way. Perhaps Jerónimo was right and all Rosita had ever needed was a firm hand, only she couldn't help wishing it wasn't what he obviously thought she was in need of too! It was years and years since anyone had thought her foolish and irresponsible. And female, a little voice whispered inside her. He thought her female all right, and she hadn't made up her mind yet whether she liked that or not, for female, to Jerónimo, meant helpless and subservient and all sorts of other things, whereas, to her, it meant equal but different. Quite definitely different, as was brought home to her every time she spent a few minutes in his company, but *that* she preferred not to think about at all!

A knock on her bedroom door made her finish her packing in a flurry.

'May I come in?' Jerónimo's voice asked.

'Yes.' She busied herself with the catches of the suitcase, struggling to maintain a calm front, which became more and more difficult as he stood in front of her, watching her.

'Let me see,' he said. 'Perhaps they are rusty from lack of use.'

He knelt down beside her and snapped the suitcase shut with one easy movement, sending her a mocking glance at the same time. Perhaps female did mean helpless, she thought, feeling more hot and bothered than ever.

'Thank you,' she said.

A muscle tugged in the side of his face. 'It was a pleasure!'

Rachel restrained herself from landing the suitcase a harassed kick. 'Where's Rosita—' she said instead.

'Making some tea. She suggested she should make coffee, but—' he barely suppressed a shudder – 'she makes such terrible coffee that I thought you would prefer tea.'

Meaning that he would! Rachel suppressed a smile. 'Her tea isn't much better!' she commented.

But, as always when she criticized her sister, Jerónimo defended the younger girl. 'You should have allowed her to do her share in the kitchen,' he said stiffly. 'She tells me that neither you nor Carmen would allow her to do any of the cooking.'

' "Allow"?' Rachel murmured. 'I've never thought of it that way.'

Jerónimo eyed her thoughtfully. 'Did Carmen do the cooking?' he asked.

'No.'

He looked amused. 'Wouldn't you "allow" her in the kitchen either?' he asked.

'Well, naturally, she took all her orders from me,' Rachel began, and then ended hastily, 'It was too much trouble! You know how it was with Carmen!'

'And how old were you?' he countered.

'Not very old – but old enough!' she insisted.

He picked up her suitcase and placed it beside Rosita's three cases in the hall. 'You will find things very different in Granada,' he told her. 'Is this all the luggage you're taking?' And then, when Rachel nodded, 'You obviously believe in travelling light?'

Rachel didn't like to tell him that that one suitcase held everything she possessed in the world. She had never had many clothes and in the last six months she had cut her wardrobe down to the bare bones in an effort to economize.

'I don't need much,' she explained.

To her relief he accepted that without comment. He glanced at his watch and smiled at her. 'It will have to be rather a quick cup of tea,' he said. 'Do you mind?'

Rachel thought Rosita was looking decidedly subdued when she brought in the tea-tray and poured out the three cups of tea. There were shadows beneath her eyes and she looked very much as though she might have been crying.

'Are you all right?' she asked as she accepted the cup the younger girl handed her.

Rosita screwed up her face. 'I don't want to go to Spain after all!' she burst out. 'Not if you're going! You spoil everything, just because you're older than I am!'

'But, Rosita darling—'

'I *hate* you!' Rosita sobbed.

Rachel looked away, trying to hide the hurt that her sister had dealt her. It was not a mood she knew how to cope with, familiar though it was. Rosita was given to sudden storms of temperament and she never cared what she said during one of her tantrums. Rachel had known long since that she was a fool to allow herself to be hurt, but hurt she was.

'It's nothing to do with me,' she said, the back of her throat stiff with humiliation that Jerónimo should be witnessing such a scene.

'You din't have to write to *him*!' Rosita cast an eloquent glance in her cousin's direction. 'My family has nothing to do with you!'

Jerónimo whirled round before Rachel could answer. 'Rosita! Don't ever let me hear you say such a thing again!' he bit out. 'You will apologize to your sister at once!'

'It doesn't matter,' Rachel interposed hastily.

Jerónimo silenced her with a look '*Al contrario*, it matters very much. It has been difficult enough to persuade you that you are family without Rosita undoing all the good work I have done on you—'

Rachel stiffened. 'If that's all that's worrying you—'

'Oh, *hija*, do you have to take it in turns to be difficult? It will be better when you both come to terms with your new life and accept that you can't always do exactly as you like. Now, we'll hear no more about it!'

Rachel took a sip of tea, a little bewildered to find herself in the wrong again. 'I can see it would suit you very well to have us do everything you tell us without a word of protest, but we weren't brought up that way—'

'Raquel!'

Rachel subsided into silence, but the look she gave him spoke volumes for the restraint she was imposing on herself.

'Rachel,' he said again in low tones, standing over her in a way that made her spill her tea in the saucer. It would have gone down her skirt too if he hadn't taken it away from her and put it down on the table beside her. 'Of course it was the way you were brought up! You forget that I knew Carmen too.'

His eyes held hers. 'But not Rosita!' she told him. 'It was always different for her!'

'We're not talking about Rosita, we're talking about you.'

Her eyes fell. 'Carmen was more than a mother to me,' she confessed. 'She was a friend. But someone had to try and hold things together after they – they died. There was no one else.'

'There was me!' Rosita said with a tinkling little laugh. 'Nobody asked you to make a martyr of yourself! We all told you that – especially Duncan,' she added maliciously. 'Duncan was Rachel's boy-friend,' she rattled on. 'But he gave her up when she decided she had to work in the evenings as well. I went out with him for a bit after that, but he was terribly dull and he couldn't dance for toffee-nuts—'

'And you allowed that?' Jerónimo demanded of Rachel.

She cleared her throat, remembering the misery she had felt when she had first known that Rosita had been seeing Duncan. 'I suppose so,' she managed. 'He's a very reliable person.'

Jerónimo said nothing. He didn't have to. Rachel knew exactly what he was thinking and she didn't like it one bit.

She wished that she had never heard of Duncan, had never half-wondered if she were in love with him, and more than ever that Rosita hadn't chosen to mention his name now so that Jerónimo could destroy her much cherished memories of him in a brutal silence.

'He was nice,' she said.

Jerónimo drew himself up with decision. 'You won't be seeing him again, nice or not, while you are in Spain, so you had better forget all about him!'

Rachel lifted her chin. 'Carmen liked him too!' she declared.

Jerónimo was unimpressed. He drank his tea standing, his eyes never leaving Rachel's face. She tried to ignore him and picked up her own cup again, but she could not. No one had ever looked at her in quite that way before or, if they had, they had had the grace to look away when she had caught them at it. But Jerónimo didn't mind what effect he had on her. He studied the lines of her blouse, the bright fairness of her hair, and the soft, determined curves of her mouth, with a casual amusement that raised a storm of rebellion within her. She would have loved to have told him what she thought of him, but she dared not, and that added to her humiliation at his hands. Despite herself, she couldn't resist looking at him and, as their eyes met, he raised his eyebrows in an expression of pure mockery that shattered her composure. If he could look at her, why shouldn't she look at him? But when she did, she found herself remembering how his lips had felt against hers and she was more afraid than ever that he would be able to read her mind and would despise her because she hadn't disliked his kiss at all.

'I don't think I should have liked him,' he said, 'and any future friends you have will have me to deal with. They won't find it easy to pull the wool over my eyes, and nor will you, little Raquel. This Duncan of yours is not worth a thought from either of you!'

Rachel pressed her lips together. 'Just because he's an

Englishman—' she began.

'So you do remember that you are destined to marry a Spaniard?' he taunted her. 'Keep on remembering that, *pequeña*, and you won't come to any harm!'

'I prefer Englishmen,' she asserted firmly.

He bent forward and ran a finger down her straight, sensible nose. 'Do you indeed?' he mocked her. 'I think not!' His mood changed with a lightning suddenness. 'Rosita, wash up the tea-things and put them away, there's a good girl,' he commanded. 'It's time we were going.'

Rachel remembered very little of the flight to Granada. Jerónimo took charge of everything and she floated along beside him, feeling not quite real, and not even caring whether Rosita behaved herself or not. A car took them to Heathrow where their luggage was checked in and their passports examined, Jerónimo having to go through a different barrier from the two girls. After that they were searched by the security people who hover round every departure lounge nowadays, and waited for their flight to be called. It was strange to walk straight out of the building on to the plane as if it were just another room, and stranger still to be firmly told to sit down in the window seat with Rosita beside her and not to have an argument about it. But perhaps Rosita wanted to sit next to her cousin more than she wanted to look out of the window at the changing scene below.

She had never known that Spain was such a vast country. It seemed to go on for ever, a huge expanse of wrinkled mountains, rocky plains, and the saw-like Sierras that surrounded the gem that was Granada, one of the best loved places in the world. Coming down at the airport, it was difficult to see why the Arab world had considered it the prize of all they possessed, and even harder to know why some of the descendants of the conquered Moors still treasure the heavy, old-fashioned keys to the houses they had once owned in the city they had built and which they considered the reflection of all that was best and most lavish in their glorious civilization, which in many ways is one of the greatest which the world has known. It was a small airport and they had it practically to themselves as they stepped out of the air-conditioned cabin into the bright sunshine outside.

'*Bienvenido!*' Jerónimo said as they stepped down on to Spanish soil.

'What does that mean?' Rosita asked him.

He frowned, displeased. 'Ask your sister,' he advised her. 'Really, Rosita, you will have to do better than that!'

'Well, what does it mean?' Rosita insisted.

'Welcome,' Rachel whispered to her.

'Is that all? What a fuss about nothing!' Rosita pouted up at Jerónimo, her eyes crinkling in the glare. 'I've never been able to speak Spanish,' she said carelessly. 'Mama didn't mind because she'd learned English by the time I came along.'

'You'll have to learn to speak it now. I'll arrange for you to have lessons.'

Rosita's pout took on a sulky twist. 'Rachel too?'

Jerónimo shrugged. 'If she needs them.' He gave Rachel a certain look that made her quiver inwardly. 'I shall have to find out how much she knows first. I may decide to teach her myself.'

'*Oh no!*' Rachel gasped. 'I mean, I'm sure you're busy enough without my imposing on your time. I wouldn't want to be a nuisance!'

'You'll never be that,' he assured her lazily. He gave her a push before him into the building, taking her passport out of her hand putting it with his own and Rosita's to make it easier for the immigration official.

As soon as the luggage came off the plane, they passed through Customs and pushed their way through the swing doors that led out to a waiting row of taxis and private cars that had come to meet the London plane. Rachel looked about her, intrigued by the old-fashioned look to the advertisements that met her eye. A light breeze ruffled the dust at her feet, and a tubby porter kissed his hand to her in a compliment to the unusual fairness of her hair.

'I should have thought Rosita would have been more to his taste,' she told Jerónimo, smiling.

'The little rose is well enough,' he agreed tolerantly, 'but I find you *mas guapa*. I have never seen anyone so fair before.'

More attractive! Well, he had a funny way of showing it, finding fault with everything she did! She opened her mouth indignantly, but her rebuke was stillborn as she came face to face with a woman who was so like Carmen that, for a moment, she thought her stepmother had come to life again. But of course, this woman was older, much older than Carmen despite the similarity of features and expression. Her skin had been protected from the sun by a thick layer of cream, but underneath was a wrinkled walnut. There was nothing old about the look that flashed in her fine eyes, however, as she took Jerónimo's broad frame into her arms.

'Abuela!' He kissed his grandmother warmly, lifting her right off the ground in an exuberant hug. 'How are you, Abuelita?'

'Well,' the old lady returned, somehow retaining her dignity in the midst of his embrace. 'I couldn't wait another minute to meet my two granddaughters!' She whirled out of his reach the second he set her down, laughingly pushing him away from her. 'This is Raquel, yes? And this is Rosita?' She held out her cheek for their kisses. 'How glad I am to see you both!'

'But Rachel isn't really related to you at all.' Rosita pointed out.

'Nonsense, child! Your mother was her mother too. Carmen loved her little ready-made daughter dearly, and so shall I my granddaughter. Besides, she speaks Spanish, I am told, and I was always too lazy to learn English properly, so

32

she will probably be my favourite granddaughter until you can speak your mother's language too!'

Rachel waited for the storm to break, but Rosita said nothing. She sat as far away from her grandmother in the car as she could, though, casting baleful glances in the old lady's direction whenever she thought that no one was looking.

'She is spoilt, that one,' Abuela declared in Spanish to Rachel, 'but she won't get the better of me!'

'But she is right, *señora*,' Rachel impressed on her. 'I haven't any real claim on you. I wouldn't have come, only Señor Parades insisted. But I shan't stay! I shall make sure that Rosita settles in happily and then I shall go back to England—'

'This is the one you have to watch!' Jerónimo interrupted her, smiling affectionately at his grandmother. '*Es una cara dura!* She has the cheek of the devil, and much of his independence too! I am looking to you to teach her how a young lady should behave. She thinks nothing of telling me to mind my own business whenever I make a suggestion as to what she should do!'

Abuela chuckled. 'That must be a new experience for you!' she said dryly.

'I think you might speak English when you know I can't understand a word you're saying!' Rosita complained.

'You will have to learn!' her grandmother told her.

'Jerónimo is going to arrange for me to have lessons,' she said virtuously.

'And Raquel?' Abuela asked.

'I shall teach Raquel everything she needs to know myself,' Jerónimo drawled. 'Then she can't complain that her new family is neglecting her! What are you doing in Granada, *abuelita*? Nothing wrong, I hope?'

The old lady retired into herself for a moment. 'No, nothing wrong,' she said. 'I came to meet my grand-daughters, what else? I know it would be far too long before you would bring them to Casares to see me, and so I came to Granada to see them.'

Perhaps it was because Rachel was sitting so close to the old lady in the car that she felt the slight tremor that passed through the elegant frame pressed against hers. There was something wrong, she thought, and wondered a little at her own concern. But this was Carmen's mother, and so it shouldn't be a surprise to her that she should feel a warm bond between them. She turned her head a little and studied the face that was the image of what Carmen's had promised to be in old age. She noticed the lines of pain round the eyes and the tightness of the jaw and she was more sure than ever that the old lady was trying to hide something from the eagle eye of her grandson.

Abuela glanced round suddenly and their eyes met. The old lady shook her head and Rachel's eyes filled with unbidden tears. She felt her hand taken into the dry, thin hand of the Spanish lady.

'You are just as Carmen said you were, *niña*. I feel as if you were twice my granddaughter! We will have no more nonsense about you going back to England, *convenido*? You will call me Abuela, like my other grandchildren do, yes? And after a while, you may even bring yourself to call your cousin Jerónimo. Has he given you a bad time?'

Rachel lowered her voice to a whisper. 'I don't think he likes me,' she confessed. 'And I know he doesn't approve of me!'

The old lady poked her grandson in the ribs. 'Jerónimo, at last I have found a girl who doesn't find you *simpatico!*'

He turned his head, his eyes travelling slowly and deliberately up Rachel's face. 'Is that what she told you?' He turned away again. 'Don't listen to her, Abuela! She was working herself to death in England and was only too glad when I came to rescue her! She should have written to us long ago. If she tells you I was unkind to her, I can tell you a fine story about her too! Do you know *where* she was working?'

'Jerónimo, you wouldn't!' Rachel pleaded with him.

'Was it so terrible?' Abuela asked, much enjoying the exchange.

'No, it wasn't!' Rachel protested. 'I *enjoyed* working there. But Jerónimo was determined to think the worst, right from the beginning! And as if that wasn't enough, he gave in my notice at my office job too!'

'And what did Rosita do?' Abuela asked, her eye snapping.

'She's only just left school,' Rachel answered.

'I see,' the old lady said. 'Never mind, Raquel. I shan't ask where you were working if you don't want me to know. That is all in the past. Now, you have only to enjoy yourself in Spain!'

Rachel glared at the back of Jerónimo's head. 'I'm not ashamed of working as a barmaid!' she declared. 'It was a very respectable pub, and the landlord was a pet! He was very *kind* to me.'

Jerónimo turned round then. 'All the more reason for you to leave,' he said severely. 'I met him too, remember, and your other employer also. It's more than time that you had a family to look after you—'

'But not you!'

'Why not?' When she didn't answer, he reached out a hand over the back of the seat and pushed her hair back out of her eyes. 'Well, Raquel, why not?'

Rachel sought help from the old lady beside her, but Abuela, too, was all kindly inquiry. 'This is ridiculous!' Rachel managed a half-hearted tone.

They both laughed, bringing Rosita's angry interest down on her head.

'I think it is you who is ridiculous,' Jerónimo said, and he tucked her hair behind her ear and laughed again. '*Beautifully ridiculous!*'

CHAPTER THREE

IT was impossible to spend a moment longer in bed. Rachel threw back the sheet and hurried to the window to see what the view was like in daylight. To her dismay, she found she could see very little. The house had been built round a small, formal garden which normally would have been a delight to her eyes, but which that morning seemed faintly dull when she had been expecting the glories of the snow-capped mountains and the endless views that made Granada such a famous city.

She opened the latticed shutters the evening before because she liked to have as much light as possible in her room, but she noticed that none of the family had done the same. She might have been alone in the world, for no one else was up in the golden-stone building and she began to wish that she had consulted someone as to whether he was expected to get up for breakfast, or whether it would be brought to her room.

It was too nice a day not to dress and explore her new surroundings though, and the joys of having a bathroom all to herself were too great not to be used by having a quick shower before she pulled on a shirt and a pair of bright orange cotton trousers. As soon as she was ready, she crept down the corridor as silently as possible so as not to waken anyone else and slipped out of the nearest door that led out into the sunlight.

She saw immediately that it was not the door they had come in by the evening before. That had been huge, carved, and surrounded by ornate geometric patterns that might or might not have been stylized flowers and animals, but it had been difficult to see in the fading light. This door led out into yet another yard, cobbled, with a long line of stables down one side and the wall of the house on the other. The third wall was the back of someone else's house, and the fourth was taken up by an arched entrance, surmounted by the tiled portrait of the Virgin and Child.

In the middle of the yard Jerónimo was seated astride a chestnut gelding that must have stood all of seventeen hands. Already restless, the horse shied at the sight of her and was brought under control by an almost unnoticeable movement of Jerónimo's wrists.

'Good morning,' he said to her. 'I hope you slept well?'

He looked so different in his Spanish clothes, his broad-brimmed, flat-topped *sombrero ancho* set at a rakish angle on his head, and the thin black tie that called attention to the strength of his neck and jaw.

'If you want to come with me, I can wait,' he suggested, looking down at her with that familiar, mocking stare that made her so self-conscious in his presence.

'I don't know how to ride,' she confessed.

'You could learn.'

She advanced a few quick steps, her face lighting up with excitement. 'Would you teach me?' Then her face fell. 'But it would hold you up and your horse looks impatient to be off now.'

He gave her a sardonic smile. 'The horse will do as I tell it. Well, do you want to come?'

'Yes,' she said.

He dismounted, pulling the reins over his horse's head in an easy movement. 'Hold my horse, then, while I saddle up my mother's mare for you. She won't run away with you, or play you up at all. All you have to do is sit on her and let her do the rest.' He looked her up and down. 'I think a side-saddle, don't you?'

'But *nobody* rides side-saddle nowadays!' she protested.

'They do around here, especially at *ferias* and other get-togethers. Riding astride is all right for men, but women

37

weren't built for it.' His smile grew wider. 'You'll look much more elegant and attractive up on Mother's saddle!'

Rachel gave him a dying look. 'I don't think your mother would like it!'

His eyes narrowed. 'Why not?'

She licked her lips, remembering her reception by Señora Parades the evening before. Jerónimo's mother was quite unlike those who had been born into the Parades family. Abuela had told her that she favoured the Lucot family, who were all small and dumpy, just as the Parades were tall and black-eyed. Together they summed up the two distinct types of Spaniard. But Rachel had been far more aware of the hostility with which her hostess had greeted her. Rosita she had been prepared to tolerate, as Carmen's daughter and her husband's niece. Rachel's coming was a penance that she was only prepared to accept under protest. In faultless English, she had suggested that Rosita should address her as Tia Nicolasa and then, more slowly, she had gone on to Rachel, 'I think my son would consider Señora too formal, Miss Andrews, so shall we agree that you will call me Doña Nicolasa?'

Jerónimo patted his horse's neck. 'This is my house, Raquel,' he said. 'It would be a mistake to believe that anyone else is master here. My mother knows that as well as anyone.'

'Isn't that rather old-fashioned?' she retorted.

'It's the way it is. When my father was alive, everyone, including myself, accorded to his wishes, but now it is I who have the responsibility of being the head of the family and who makes the decisions for all of us.'

'And you expect everyone to obey you, I suppose?' she flashed at him. 'Well, I don't belong to your family, so you needn't think you can run my life for me! I've never heard anything more barbaric than for a son to order his mother about! Poor Doña Nicolasa!'

'Don't waste your sympathy,' Jerónimo advised her

38

dryly. 'My mother is the centre of a loving family and is secure in her own sphere. She wouldn't thank me if I expected her to take on a man's responsibilities as well.'

Feeling a lot less sure of her ground, Rachel decided on a rearguard action. 'I pity your wife!' she declared with a violence that set the horse dancing away from her.

Jerónimo's laughter rang out across the yard. 'You may well! No wife of mine will rule my inheritance, or me either! On the other hand, she would be much loved and I know well how to protect my own, so it might be a lesson she would learn willingly. What do you think?'

He brought the whole of his personality to bear on her and she blinked, not knowing what to say. A sharp shaft of envy shot through her, though she would not admit to herself that it was any such thing. How could he be so sure of himself?

'I think you'd better marry a Spanish woman,' she managed. 'No English woman would put up with it!'

'No?' His eyes mocked her. 'We'll have to see. Meanwhile, you may use my mother's saddle because I say so, and not worry about anything else. Yes?'

He saddled up the mare with the same efficiency with which he did everything else, taking the reins of his own horse from her and hooking them over a nearby post. Rachel approached the mounting block with some trepidation, but he seemed so sure that she would manage to ride the mare that some of his confidence seeped into her and she felt quite perky when he lifted her into the saddle and taught her how to lock her right knee into position.

'Don't hold on for dear life!' he commanded. 'There's no surer way of falling off! And sit up straight!' He took a step back and surveyed her with approval. 'That's *much* better!'

'But I can't move!' Rachel objected.

'You don't have to move, except to sway a little with the movement of the horse. Now, we shall walk slowly round the yard to give you the feel of it, and then we'll go for our ride.'

'You mean I'll be on my own?' she gasped.

'No, no,' he assured her. 'I'll have you on a leading rein.' He began to walk the mare forward. 'Are you enjoying yourself?' he asked after a while.

'*Es estupendo!*' she answered sarcastically.

He urged the mare into a trot. 'Good!' he commended Rachel. 'In Spanish too! You're coming on, little one!'

'Don't you mean coming off?'

He turned his head to look at her. 'Sit up straight! If you sit there like a sack, of course you will lose your balance. Don't look so scared, Raquel. It's very difficult to fall out of a side-saddle.'

They slowed to a walk and he corrected the way she was holding the reins, his strong, firm fingers forcing her hands into the approved position. 'You see, it's not difficult!' He pushed his hat a little further back on his head. 'If you do well, *hija*, I'll let you ride to the next *feria* – or take you up behind me on my horse. You'll enjoy that.'

He swung himself back into the saddle, leaned forward to catch up her leading rein and turned both horses towards the archway and the open spaces beyond. 'Come on now, hold your head up! You must look as proud as a true Spanish *señorita*, or everyone will know it's your first time up on a horse!'

'The Andrews can be as proud as any Spaniard!' she said fiercely, squaring her shoulders to ease the aching muscles at the base of her spine. 'You can let the leading rein go if you want to go on ahead. I'll be quite all right by myself!'

'Not yet, *pequeña*, not yet!' He jerked the rein, making the mare come up close beside him. 'Not until you've grown used to having my hand on the reins.' He raised an eyebrow at her indignant face. 'Both on and off a horse,' he added maliciously. 'And *don't* lose your temper! It won't do you any good and you'll lose the rhythm of what you are doing!'

Her eyes kindled. 'Are you trying to be beastly?'

'Not at the moment. At this moment, I am only interested in turning you into an adequate equestrienne, but if you have other ideas, you have only to say and I'll do my best to oblige you!'

'I don't know what you mean,' she said stiffly.

He leaned across, picking her hands off the mare's neck with a reproachful look. 'I think you do,' he tormented her. He sat up straight, smiling to himself. 'Shall we canter, my pretty one, or have you had enough?'

'I'd be scared to canter—'

'I won't let you go!'

The trembling within her burst into a fountain of warm excitement. 'Then – then I'd like to – if you think I can?'

It seemed to her that they flew across the ground. She settled more firmly into her borrowed saddle and made the most of the wind whipping her hair against her face, trying to remember all that Jerónimo had told her: to sit up straight; to hold her head and her hands up; and to allow the bottom half of her body to sway gently with the rhythm of the horse's movement. It was a marvellous sensation!

'That was wonderful!' she enthused as their pace steadied back to a walk.

'This is one of my favourite places,' he told her. 'From here you can see the whole city spread out beneath your feet.' He dismounted, tying his horse to a nearby tree, and reached out his arms to her to lift her down beside him. She made a little gesture of dismissal, to tell him that she would rather stay where she was, but he gave her no choice, grasping her round the waist and lifting her high, lowering her to her feet so slowly that she was more than ever conscious of his strength of arm and body, and the sheer majestic height of the man. She stumbled a little when he let her go and hurried away to a safe distance where she wouldn't feel his breath on her face, or the warmth of his body against hers.

'Does the snow stay on the mountains all the year round?'

she asked.

'Here and there. In the winter, the skiing is very good and people come from all over Spain for the winter sports. My brother is very keen and we have high hopes that he will soon be up to international competition.'

'I didn't know you had a brother,' Rachel said.

'Diego is my only brother. I have a sister too, but we see her less often now since she married and went to live in Madrid.'

'Is Diego like you?'

Jerónimo looked amused. 'He is like Mama – small and well covered! You will not be at all afraid of *him*.'

Rachel threw back her head. 'I'm not at all afraid of you!'

'Not at this moment,' he agreed. 'What do you think of my beautiful city?'

Rachel thought it was the most fantastic sight she had ever seen. The Alhambra, the most ancient Arab part of the city, stood in golden splendour on an outcrop of solid rock that was partially covered by trees. On one side was the Rio Darro that disappeared underground after a while, and on the other was the Rio Genil. Closer still, almost directly below them, was the rest of the city, crumbling at the edges to make way for new roads and the new blocks of flats that are part of the modern impedimenta of every modern suburb.

'Don't you ever feel sorry for the Moors who were driven out of their homes?' she said aloud.

'Often,' he admitted. 'They can never be forgotten here. Did you know that the Catholic kings—'

'Isabella and Ferdinand?'

He nodded. 'They chose to be buried in the cathedral here, but their monument can't compare with that of their predecessors, despite the care they lavished on it.'

'May one visit the Alhambra?' she asked him eagerly.

'Of course. We live near enough for you to visit every day

if you so wish. Only the first time I shall take you myself and show you all the wonders there are to be seen and which are part of the history of every Grenadine. Will you come with me?'

She felt as though he were offering her the keys to the city itself. Her pleasure was a living thing within her, and she lowered her gaze so that he wouldn't see how much his offer meant to her.

'I'd like that,' she said.

When she did look up, she found he was staring at her with an unreadable expression in his eyes. His face was stern and his nostrils flared as if he were controlling himself only with difficulty. Oh dear, she thought, somehow she had managed to do the wrong thing again! And she had so wanted his approval at that particular moment, though why, she could not have said.

'Shouldn't we be going back?' she suggested, horrified to discover that she was close to tears.

He put a hand on the small of her back and turned her to face him, touching her cheek with a gentle finger. 'What soft skin you have,' he said, just as though she hadn't spoken at all. 'We must find you a hat to protect it from the sun.'

'A hat like yours?' Her voice trembled, betraying the melting weakness she felt within her.

'A hat like mine,' he confirmed. He ran his finger down her nose and traced the generous curves of her mouth with a thoughtful air. 'I suppose you use all sorts of creams and lotions—'

'I do not!' she retorted.

'No? Then how do you keep it so smooth and soft?'

Her answer caught in the back of her throat. 'I don't do anything—' she began, but his finger silenced her. 'Jerónimo?'

The hand on her back drew her closer to him and he smiled. But then, with a suddenness that hurt her, he stepped away from her and put his hands in his pockets, shaking his head at her.

'It is too soon to dally with you like this, *infanta*. The Spanish air goes all too easily to a young English girl's head and she will promise a great many things she doesn't mean at all!'

'I haven't promised anything!' she denied indignantly.

'Everything about you is a promise,' he mocked her. 'But think how much you would dislike it to find yourself in the traditional female position of having to please some man to gain your happiness. You must choose your victims more carefully, *amada*, before you lose that treasured independence of yours! *I* shall never kneel at *your* feet, no matter what charms you use on me!'

'Oh, conceit!' she breathed. 'What makes you think I am trying to charm you? I don't even *like* you!'

He looked amused. 'Liking comes a lot later on – if ever!'

'You shouldn't judge others by yourself!' she told him hotly. '*I* don't victimize people, nor do I think myself so marvellous that anyone would *want* to kneel at my feet. I'm not so silly! And don't tell me I'm *beautifully* ridiculous again—'

'I shouldn't dream of it,' he cut her off.

'Oh,' she said, nonplussed.

'Yes, *oh!*' he repeated. He lifted her casually and threw her up into her saddle, handing her her reins. 'Your independence is a poor thing, my dear, and you have much to learn before you'll suit me! Meanwhile, I'd better take you home and see what tantrums your sister has in store for me.' He reached up and patted her cheek. '*You* are not permitted to have tantrums, little one. You are far too beautiful for me to be stern with you for long and you don't relish crossing swords with me, do you? Come, admit that you like it far better when I compliment you and treat you like a woman?'

Rachel sat up very straight and stared over his head

into the distance. 'I haven't noticed many compliments—' she began.

'But you have noticed that I am a man and that I find you a desirable woman!' he said dryly. He put his hand under her chin and forced her to look down at him. 'You've noticed that?'

'I could hardly help noticing you're a man!' she countered. 'I'm sure the entire female population has been only too ready to tell you that you're *muy hombre*, and all the rest of it. I happen to think other things are more important—'

His eyes held hers and her heart began to beat like thunder against her ribs. 'Like what?' he asked her so quietly that she had to strain her ears to hear him.

'Like being kind and – and considerate. Things like that!'

'And you think I'm not?'

'I think you're unbearably bossy!' she burst out.

'Is that all?'

'And far too sure of yourself!' she added:

The fire in his eyes singed her. 'Is that all?' he encouraged her. She nodded, feeling that she had gone too far already. 'Good,' he said gently. 'Because now I can tell you what I think of you—'

'No, don't, Jerónimo!'

He raised his eyebrows. 'Afraid?'

She nodded again. 'I shouldn't have said that about you. I'm sorry.'

'Where's that independence now?' he teased her. 'I expected you to pretend that you didn't care a jot what I thought of you?'

'I don't!'

To her dismay, he laughed. 'It was nothing very bad, Raquel, *mi amada*! Only a warning that I'm not only bossy and sure of myself; I don't share what is mine with anyone else! And that you have the loveliest skin I've ever seen on

45

man, woman, or child. Guard it well.'

She shrugged her shoulders. 'I don't see what your being possessive has to do with me,' she objected. 'You don't own me!'

He turned away, mounting his own horse with an ease she could only envy. 'Not yet!' he said. He picked up her leading-rein, looking over his shoulder at her with such affectionate derision that her heart stood still and then rushed into a frenzy of anxious activity. 'Not yet,' he repeated, 'but I shall!'

Of course he had meant nothing! Rachel would have been a fool if she had taken him seriously, but she felt quite weak at the knees at the very thought of the way he had stroked her face and had looked as if he would have liked to have kissed her. She tried telling herself that she was glad he had not, but the ubiquitous memory of that other time when he had kissed her, no matter how briefly, made her wonder at her own foolishness. He was more than *muy hombre*, she told herself solemnly. He was much more than that! He was the most attractive man she had ever met and, if she were not very careful, she would be allowing him liberties – But that was the most *beautifully* ridiculous thought she had had yet! She wouldn't 'allow' Jerónimo anything! He would ignore her, or command her compliance, just as the mood took him and, far from hating him for it, as instinct told her she should, she was as proud as a peacock that he had noticed her in the first place!

'Rachel!'

'*Si, señora*!' She jumped to her feet, annoyed that it should be Jerónimo's mother to catch her day-dreaming.

'Doña Nicolasa,' the older woman corrected her. 'I was expecting to find Rosita with you. Do you know where she is?'

'Jerónimo called her into his study. He's determined that she'll understand what he has done about the management of Carmen's *hacienda* and the rest of the estate, but I think he's having an uphill battle!'

Doña Nicolasa sighed. 'She's too young,' she excused her niece. 'Besides, it's quite unnecessary that she should understand such things. Jerónimo will go on managing them for her until she marries.' She hesitated, and then she said, 'It's a large estate. It would make Rosita a very good match for my son. They are first cousins, of course, but such alliances have been known before.'

'Rosita is far too young to be thinking of marriage!' Rachel murmured, shocked by her own devastation at the idea.

'Naturally, you would say that!' Doña Nicolasa smiled. 'You forget she is half Spanish. I think she would do very well for Jerónimo. She is young enough to be moulded to his ways, whereas an older girl would be fighting him all the time, and there is nothing more tiresome than a constant dispute going on in the house.' She paused to allow her words to sink in well. 'Would you like me to show you over the house?' she asked kindly. 'It's very beautiful – one of the best known in the whole of Granada! You'll know better then why Jerónimo can expect a great deal from his wife. No bride has come empty-handed to their marriage in our family for more than a hundred years and, probably, for a great deal longer than that! Did your father leave you a dowry? Or your mother? But then you have no need to worry, have you? Such considerations are thought very much behind the times in England, I believe?'

'It's considered more important that they should be happy,' Rachel returned evenly.

Doña Nicolasa showed her teeth in a smile. 'We have no divorce rate yet in Spain!' she pointed out.

'It varies from family to family in England. We have never had a divorce in my family either!'

'So?' Doña Nicolasa sounded surprised. 'Jerónimo says your Spanish is very good,' she went off at a tangent. 'If

Carmen took the trouble to teach you, why didn't she teach her own daughter?'

Rachel was embarrassed. 'Rosita hasn't much aptitude for languages,' she explained.

Doña Nicolasa bit her lip in annoyance. 'The most Spanish thing about her are her looks!' Her eyes twinkled suddenly, giving her a much more friendly appearance. 'The same can hardly be said of you! No Spaniard ever had blonde hair such as yours, yet we don't hear a word from you that the sun is too hot and that you are lonely because no one will speak English to you!'

'I like it here,' Rachel confessed.

'Does Rosita?'

'She will in time. It's strange to her at first. You'll have to give her time, Doña Nicolasa. I'm sure she'll settle down happily enough in the end.'

'I hope you may be right.' The Spanish woman's face was crumpled with anxiety and she looked suddenly older than her years. 'I can't pretend that Carmen's daughter is anything other than a disappointment to me. She comes and goes as she pleases, without a word to anyone, and Jerónimo holds me responsible for seeing that she conforms to the ways of the household. And you, you are no better! Where were you this morning when the maid took your breakfast to your room?'

'I went riding with Jerónimo,' Rachel said faintly.

'And after that?'

Rachel thought she could hardly say that she had been keeping out of Jerónimo's mother's way ever since Jerónimo had commandeered both her mare and her saddle for Rachel's use. She had spent most of her time in her room. Then she remembered with relief that she had also spent an hour or so with Abuela, helping her to fit a dress she was making.

'Abuela—'

'Did she tell you to call her that?'

Rachel nodded. 'I know she isn't my grandmother, but she is my step-grandmother and she seems to think that counts!'

'Your step-great-grandmother,' Doña Nicolasa corrected her with an odd little smile. 'Carmen was her eldest granddaughter. Her mother married much younger than any of her sisters. It was sad for Carmen that she came between generations, not old enough to find her friends amongst her uncles' wives, nor young enough to play with her own cousins. There was all of ten years between her and Jerónimo. Perhaps that is why she went to England and found her happiness there – if she did!'

Rachel didn't answer. She was wise enough to know that the implied slight to her father had probably not been intended and that, anyway, now was not the time to defend her parent. If anything, she was rather amused to find that Spanish stereotyped prejudices about the English were quite as ill-founded and probably of just as long-standing as those of the English for the Spanish.

'You promised to show me over the house,' Rachel reminded the older woman, hoping to turn her mind to happier matters. 'What I've seen of it so far, it's very beautiful!'

This struck exactly the right note to put Doña Nicolasa in the best of good humours. The house was her hobby as well as her home and she adored every stick and stone of it.

'We are fortunate in Granada to still have many of the old ancestral, aristocratic mansions left. You will see some of the most famous as you walk about the old part of the city: grand houses such as the Casa de los Tires; Casa de Castril; and the Casa del Padre Suarez. This house is not as famous as any of those, of course, though I like to think it is only because we are right on the edge of the city. The earliest part of the house was built at about the same time as the buildings of the Alhambra, which has given a very Moorish flavour to the layout. We call the little walled-in gardens

49

carmens – your room looks over one of them, but there are several others within the bounds of the house.'

'It's very pretty,' Rachel commented.

'They are beautiful! Pretty is too frivolous a term for them, not melancholy enough! The Grenadines have always a touch of melancholy, even when they are most content. This has been so in every age. Much of this house was rebuilt by the Christians at the time of the Reconquest – mostly the baroque and Renaissance parts – but see how well it harmonizes with the Arab and Mudejar styles. This interlacery roofing is Moorish. We have it in many of our public rooms, most of which are interconnected by little courtyards. That arcade is supported by cubic capitals on Nazari columns. Do you find it beautiful? Or is it too oriental to your English eyes?'

Rachel looked about her with appreciation. 'I find it paradise,' she said.

For once her words met with the complete approval of her hostess. 'That is what Boabdil said to Ferdinand and Isabella when he surrendered the city to them in 1492. He was the last Moorish sultan of Granada. Perhaps you have heard of him? No? He was very young and very sad. "Here," he said, "are the keys to Paradise." This is what Granada is to every one of us.' She glanced at Rachel, her expression wry. 'But will it ever be that to Rosita?'

CHAPTER FOUR

'ONE might just as well live in a museum!' Rosita brooded. 'I'd give anything to be back in that horrid flat we had in London! Rachel, I'm terribly homesick. Can't we possibly go home?'

'Of course we can't!' The very idea gave Rachel a lowering feeling. How unfair life was, she thought. Here was she, happier than she had ever been in her life, when Rosita, who should have been blossoming in her new life, was not only homesick but was beginning to look decidedly peaky as well. 'You know we can't! You'll get used to living here, Rosita, and then you'll wonder what you were making such a fuss about. It's your inheritance after all!'

'I hate it!' Rosita said gloomily. 'I absolutely hate it! And that awful woman keeps looking at me as though she wanted Jerónimo to eat me up, and as for him, I can never think of anything to say to him. Who cares what's happening at some ghastly *hacienda* I've never seen!'

'Oh dear,' sighed Rachel.

'It's all right for you!' her sister went on in passionate tones. '*You* can understand what they're saying to you. I can't even do that!'

'But you'll soon learn enough Spanish to get by—'

'*Never*!' Rosita's mouth set in a stubborn line. 'I don't want to,' she added unanswerably.

'But you have to try!' Rachel pleaded with her.

'Why? I shan't stay here a minute longer than I have to. I'm going straight back to England, where I don't have to look at that beastly sun shrivelling everything up all day!'

'It'll rain in the winter!'

'It *floods* in the winter!' Rosita retorted.

Rachel tried another tack. 'I thought you were getting on

51

better with Abuela,' she said. 'And even if you're not, she's going back to her own house in Casares tomorrow.'

Rosita was unimpressed. 'Abuela isn't important. She's too old to have much say in anything. It's Tía Nicolasa who gives me the willies. She's always plotting to get her own way, but she never comes directly out with it. Oh, no! She treats Jerónimo as though he were some kind of king, with herself helping to put down a permanent palace revolution led by the rest of us!'

Rachel laughed. 'Jerónimo has a pretty good conceit of himself without any help from her!'

'But he doesn't play politics all the time. He just dishes out orders,' Rosita said witheringly. 'I don't mind that so much, but I do mind Tía Nicolasa looking at me as if I were a canary being specially fattened by her before the cat swallows me!'

'I think she would like you to marry Jerónimo,' Rachel admitted, feeling a little sick inside.

'She'll be lucky!' Rosita burst into hysterical laughter. 'Can you imagine me as the Parades brood mare, which is all that Jerónimo's wife will ever be? I don't even like children – in fact, I don't intend to have any! Why should I add to the population explosion?'

'Rosita!'

'Now I've shocked you!' Rosita looked more pleased than repentant. 'Oh, Rachel, really! Mama did a much better job in brainwashing you than she did on me. If only Tía Nicolasa knew it, you'd make a much better wife for Jerónimo. You'd be perfectly happy loving someone to the exclusion of everything else. I really think you'd find it quite *normal* to take second place to your husband for the rest of your life!'

'Someone has to make the decisions,' Rachel objected.

'So Mama was always saying,' Rosita reminded her, with a very knowing and adult look in her eyes. 'And a sillier saying I've never heard! As if Father was ever able to make up his mind about anything! And because Mama wouldn't make his decisions for him, we lurched from crisis to crisis, getting deeper and deeper into debt.'

'Jerónimo seems decisive enough,' Rachel said in hollow tones.

Rosita threw her a contemptuous look. 'That's the whole point! So am I! I mean to make my own decisions, and if my husband cares to go along with them that'll be all right with me!'

'But supposing he wants something different, or his job takes him somewhere you don't want to go?' Rachel felt sure she ought to take a stronger line with her young sister, but she felt quite helpless in the face of Rosita's angry confidence in her powers to run her own life. She felt even more helpless when she saw Rosita's superior smile.

'He'll have to choose between his job, or whatever, and me! I probably shouldn't like him in the first place if he didn't choose me!' Rosita added with a gay insolence that won her the argument. Her eyes snapped with malicious amusement as she looked up at her sister. 'Poor Rachel, you've never really known me at all, have you? I may look like a Palades, but I'm an Andrews through and through! I guess you took after your own mother because you'd never think we shared the same father.'

'Father wasn't hard!' Rachel defended him.

'And I am?' Rosita demanded. 'Well, maybe I am, but I'm like him in other ways. I'm bone selfish, for a start. No one could ever accuse *you* of being selfish. You have such old-fashioned ideas about these things!'

Rachel cleared her throat, trying not to laugh. 'You'll get more old-fashioned yourself as you get older!' she teased her sister.

But Rosita only shook her head. 'I mean to be Number One—'

'You do now!' Rachel agreed. 'But, Rosita, a man like Jerónimo would never allow himself to be commanded by his wife, and you wouldn't want a lesser man, would you?'

Rosita examined her fingernails with a slight frown of displeasure. 'You're such a fool, darling,' she drawled. 'Jerónimo doesn't present me with any kind of challenge at all, and if you want to know, I'd bore him into an early grave if he had to have much to do with me. Even when I *try*, he thinks I'm doing my best to be tiresome, and I don't understand a word he says!'

Rachel was shocked. 'You shouldn't rub him up the wrong way,' she began. 'He has the right to tell us what to do—'

'Speak for yourself!' Rosita interrupted, tossing her head. '*You* wrote to him, begging him to get us out of hock!'

'But you wanted to come to Spain. You *said* you did!'

'Not with you,' Rosita returned coolly. 'If I'd come by myself, they'd have soon decided that they'd rather pay through the nose to have me out of their way in England, but with you here there's no hope of that! If you can be everything they'd wanted Carmen's daughter to be, then there's hope for me yet. Only there isn't, if you see what I mean?'

'You mean you *planned* for them to dislike you?'

'More or less.'

'But they don't dislike you. It's me they dislike because I don't belong here. Even – even Jerónimo gets at me because I don't look Spanish like – like the rest of you.'

'Abuela doesn't dislike you,' Rosita contradicted.

Rachel's face softened. 'No, but she's the only one who's made me welcome. Do you know she said she felt I was twice her granddaughter? It didn't mean anything, but it was nice of her. I'll be sorry when she goes home to Casares. I can talk to her as I used to talk to Carmen.'

'And I never could!' Rosita interposed. 'Oh, don't look so guilty, Rachel. You can't help being a nicer person than I am! I like being me, and I wouldn't change places with you if I could. You may be nicer, but I have a much better time being wicked, and a minx, and not learning a word of Spanish!'

'Rosita, I could box your ears—'

'But you won't, so suppose you stop looking like an over-anxious mother hen and tell me why you're all dressed up in your Sunday best?'

Rachel flushed. If she'd had her wits about her, she thought in increasing consternation, she would have noticed that her sister was still dressed in a pair of shabby jeans and a shirt she had inherited from herself and which was much too tight for her across the bust.

'You're not ready! But Jerónimo said he wouldn't wait! You haven't forgotten that he said he was taking us to the Alhambra this afternoon?'

'I'm not going,' Rosita told her.

'But you have to come! I can't go with him by myself!'

'Why ever not?' Rosita's bland calm only served to fuel the flames of Rachel's disquiet.

'Doña Nicolasa wouldn't like it.' Rachel's mouth felt dry. 'She doesn't like it that Jerónimo is teaching me to ride—'

'But you've only been out riding with him once!'

Rachel gave her a harassed look. 'Once was enough! He accused me of flirting with him! He'll never get the opportunity to accuse me of that again!'

'Well, I'm sorry, but I'm not going to look at another old museum even for you!' Rosita said positively. 'You'll have to go on your own.' She grinned suddenly. 'If he gets out of line, why don't you slap his face for him? He'd probably die of surprise if you did!'

Rachel sat down quickly, feeling weak at the knees. 'So would I!' she declared. 'He'd probably slap me back!'

'Try it and see,' Rosita advised, sucking in her cheeks and switching her hair from one side of her face to the other to see which she preferred. 'You'd better hurry up if you don't want to keep him waiting. You're five minutes late now!'

'*Please* come!' Rachel begged, getting reluctantly to her feet.

'Not on your life, pet!' said Rosita.

Five minutes wasn't very late, Rachel assured herself as she raced through one courtyard after another to the main hall. Besides, if she had to be late, it would be far better to arrive looking cool and nonchalant, but that was beyond her and she knew it. She made a final dash along the last few feet of corridor and took a deep breath to steady herself before making her entrance, her head held high, and her breathing under strict control in case he should notice that she had been hurrying and take it as a compliment to himself.

Jerónimo was talking to his mother. Doña Nicolasa gave Rachel an angry look and turned back to her son. 'I could have taken her – or Abuela – or anyone! Why does it have to be you?'

'Because I wish to take her myself.' He, too, turned and looked at Rachel up and down. 'Do we go alone? Where is Rosita?'

'We don't have to go today!'

He raised a thoughtful eyebrow. 'That would be a pity after you have taken the trouble to change your dress, no?'

'Rosita should go with you!' Doña Nicolasa burst out. 'Where is the girl?'

'She doesn't enjoy sightseeing,' Rachel tried to explain. 'I'm sorry,' she added.

Jerónimo shrugged. 'Why should you be sorry? We shall manage very well without her.' His dark eyes mocked her worried face. 'Are you afraid to be alone with me? I thought the English would dare anything!'

'Of course not!' she said primly.

Doña Nicolasa made an explosive noise between her teeth. 'It's not Rachel you should be taking to the Alhambra. Naturally, she wishes to see all that is famous in Spain while she is here, but other arrangements can be made for that. It is Rosita who will be *living* here, who is one of us!'

Rachel stole a glance at Jerónimo. He looked bored, but

the glint in his eyes as they caught hers and held them was not bored at all.

'Are you ready, Raquel?' he asked.

'Yes,' she said.

Jerónimo started her on her way across the hall to the front door before turning to have a last word with his mother. 'Rosita is Carmen's daugher,' he murmured in Spanish, 'but Raquel is my personal guest, Mama. I shouldn't like it if she was made to feel that she was not equally welcome here.'

Doña Nicolasa flushed an unbecoming red at the criticism of her good manners, but she recovered herself nobly. 'I apologize if Rachel has had any cause for complaint,' she said stiffly.

Oh dear, Rachel thought, the older woman would never forgive her for this. She had already learned that you could criticise a Spaniard for anything, but never for a lack of manners. Certainly not an aristocrat such as Doña Nicolasa undoubtedly was! Rachel went blindly back to where Jerónimo's mother was standing.

'How could I complain, *señora*?' she said, also in Spanish. 'You have been more than kind to me and, I hope, not entirely for Carmen's sake—'

Doña Nicolasa put her arms round her and kissed her on either cheek with impulsive warmth. 'Of course not, child, you are more than welcome for yourself. I hope you will stay for a long, long time!'

Rachel released herself and, without looking at Jerónimo, preceded him out of the front door. He put his hand on her arm, but she flung it off, now thoroughly angry with him.

'How could you be so unkind?' she demanded, rubbing her arm where he had touched her.

'How could you interfere in something which was none of your business?' he retorted.

She looked at him then, her eyes wide with disbelief.

'But your mother has been kind – in her own way!'

'For her own reasons. Leave it, Raquel. This is something you can know nothing about and 'it's' not fitting that you should. My mother and I understand one another very well. We will manage quite well without you standing between us, no matter how good your intentions!'

'But to rebuke her in front of me!' she protested. 'I don't think it was at all well done!'

He shrugged. 'It was necessary.'

'How can you say so?' Her temper bubbled over into speech. 'Doña Nicolasa will never forgive me for being there – and I don't blame her. It was me you should have put down, if you had to be unpleasant to someone! I knew she didn't want me to go out with you alone and I should have insisted that Rosita came with us! It isn't much fun being a bone of contention between you!'

'You would rather I was angry with you?' He gave her an enigmatic glance that stiffened her backbone. 'Don't be silly, Raquel!'

'*Silly*?' She was strongly tempted to put Rosita's advice into action and slap him as hard as she could. 'I am not silly!'

'You are very silly,' he contradicted in a warm, intimate tone. 'You rush into things you don't begin to understand; you have the audacity to take me to task for something which is none of your business; and now you tell me that it would mean nothing to you if I retaliated by dressing you down in the same way. You would be much better employed in making yourself an agreeable companion for the afternoon. So now we shall hear no more about my supposed iniquities and shall enjoy ourselves—'

'It is, of course, my first priority to please you!' she said sarcastically.

His black eyes openly mocked her. 'I knew you would come round to my way of thinking. It's so much more rewarding to make a success, no? I think you won't have to try

58

very hard to please me very much and that will make you happy too, *hija*. Am I right?'

Her grey eyes flashed. 'I think you are the most conceited wretch I've ever met!'

'So you keep telling me. It grows tedious with repetition. One of these days, when we know each other better, you'll be ashamed that you taunted me for being master of what is mine. You would not have me less of a man, I'm thinking!'

Rachel clutched her handbag to her as if her life depended on it. 'I expect it's just that you're not my type!' she managed to say.

His laughter resounded round her ears. 'Be very careful, *querida*. I may forget you are my guest and accept the challenge! Naturally I have already thought how pleasant it would be to make love to you, and not just a brief kiss to see if your skin can possibly be as smooth and as soft as it looks! But this afternoon we have the Alhambra to see and, at the moment, you are my guest and you have no one else to protect you, so you will please be good and not do everything you can to tempt me to find out if you wouldn't like to be loved by me!'

'You wouldn't?' Rachel breathed.

He made no answer, contenting himself with opening the door of the car and pushing her inside with no more ceremony than if she had been a parcel he was taking with him.

Rachel sat in a frozen silence, making no effort to sort out the chaos that his words had wrought inside her. The memory of the touch of his lips on hers came vividly to life and she was horrified to discover a desperate longing for him to kiss her again. It couldn't be true! It was only a passing fancy, a trick of the mind she could very well have done without, but she felt again the warmth of his arms about her and the taste of ecstasy in her mouth that she had known for that brief moment in London when he had held her and had kissed her with all the mastery she had been

59

reviling him for ever since.

Was it possible that he knew how she had felt? Could he know the physical attraction he held for her? – because it was nothing more than that. She didn't like him at all, and she never would! But then he had said that liking came a lot later on, if at all. Rachel shook herself inwardly. She was being ridiculous! She was far too old to indulge in what had to be no more than a schoolgirl crush.

Jerónimo reached a hand across and laid it over hers. 'Don't!' he commanded her. 'I will not have you despising yourself for what is natural to every woman. I should not think so well of you if you felt differently, my Raquel!'

'Felt like what?' she asked in suffocated tones. He couldn't know *that* too!

'How delightfully feminine you are!' he exclaimed. 'How else should you feel but that you want to bask in the admiration of the man of your choice? But you must remember that I am only a man and that you are very beautiful and I am more used to giving way to my desires than curbing them for the sake of a young, green girl!'

'But I—'

'—talk too much!' he finished for her. 'Now, do you want to hear about the Alhambra?'

'Yes,' she said. She supposed he must have known a great many women and she imagined that they had all been dark and beautiful; exotic Spanish lovelies, ripe and ready to fall at his feet at his lightest bidding. *As she was herself!*

'Raquel, you haven't listened to a word I've said!'

The reproach made her start. 'I'm sorry,' she said automatically. 'Jerónimo, have you loved lots of women?'

His austere expression told her she was treading on the edge of disaster. He would not take kindly to such questions from her.

'Lots and lots,' he said dryly. 'Would you rather I told you about them?'

She shook her head. 'Please tell me about the Alhambra. I

60

am listening, truly I am. And we'll be there in a minute!'

He tapped her lightly on the cheek and withdrew his hand, putting it back on the wheel. ' "*Quien no ha visto Granada, No ha visto nada*".'

'If you have not seen Granada, you've seen nothing!' Rachel translated slowly. 'But you've changed the words. I thought it was a Sevillan boast, rhyming *Sevilla* with *maravilla*?'

'Once you have seen Granada, you won't even think about Seville!' he told her. 'I shall see to that!'

'I can't compare the two because I've never been to Seville, but I mean to go one day and then I'll tell you whether it's more marvellous or not.' She chuckled. 'The Sevillans are more modest! At least they only say that he who has not seen Seville has not seen a marvel, not *nothing*!'

'Ah, but once you are a Grenadine, all else *is* as nothing!' His look was as intimate as a caress. 'You'll find out, *querida*, that paradise is dearly bought. One can't approach it with a divided heart or it doesn't work! You have been warned, it has to be all or nothing!'

She was thankful she didn't have to make such a choice. The Spanish mind was as ruthless as his scenery, she thought. The blinding sunlight caused the deep purple shadows, leaving no room for the wishy-washy colours of compromise. Well, she was prepared to fall in love with Grenada, just a little bit, because she found it so heart-satisfyingly beautiful, but she wasn't prepared to go overboard for any place under the sun. It was only then that she thought that Jerónimo might not have been talking about Grenada at all, but that conjured up such a shattering vision of possible bliss that she felt quite faint and put the whole idea resolutely out of her mind.

'Perhaps you'll prefer another description of Granada,' he broke in on her thoughts, very much to her relief. A muscle quivered in his cheek and she was almost sure that he was laughing at her, and really, she couldn't blame him! *Once*

61

she was a Grenadine – but she never would be!

' " . . . and look around you;
The city is a lady whose husband is the mountain.
The river's girdle clasps her, and the flowers
Smile like the jewels that twinkle at her throat." '

'*Oh*!' she gasped.

'Ibn Zamrak was talking about the city, not you,' he said in a snubbing tone.

'I know that! *Who* did you say?'

'Ibn Zamrak. He lived here in the fourteenth century. The Sierra Nevada was as grand in his day as it is in ours and, presumably, he thought the city just as beautiful!'

Grand the mountains certainly were. Grand, and remote, and austere enough to break a foolish heart on. And the man sitting beside her was just like them. Had Ibn Zamrak known just such a man? Yet how well they guarded the city, giving it a security it would not otherwise have had. The life of Granada, the envy of the world, would not have been possible if the Sierra Nevada had not enfolded the city and kept it safe from most of the marauders who had come to disturb her dreaming existence – and those conquerors who had come, like Ferdinand and Isabella, had left it much as they had found it. They had scarcely impinged on the love affair between the mountains and the man-made paradise they held in their grasp.

'How sad that the Moors had to leave!' she exclaimed, her eyes filling with tears.

'You should rejoice at a fine Christian victory,' he chided her. He parked the car beneath the thick trees beside the road, having negotiated the narrow way up into the Alhambra itself. He put the car-keys in his pocket, turning a little towards her. She looked away, but not quickly enough for him to miss her tears. He put up a hand and caressed the back of her neck, fingering her blonde hair until she could bear it no longer. She wiped her cheeks with the back of her hand and attempted a laugh at her own stupidity.

'It was too long ago to rejoice or mourn,' she said fiercely. 'But he loved it here, and even if he didn't have to go, his people did.'

His hand tightened on her neck as he pulled her close up against him. 'Do *you* love it here?' he murmured.

But she never had the opportunity to reply, for his mouth came down on hers and her heart somersaulted within her as she strained closer still, betrayed by her own need for him. He kissed her as though it was his right to take what he pleased from her, exploring her mouth with his own with a complete disregard for her half-hearted struggles to be free of him. Her arms crept round his neck and she rejoiced in the hardness of the muscles in his back and harsh, springing quality of his hair between her fingers.

In the next moment he had grasped her by either arm and had propelled her firmly back into her own seat. She wasn't ready to be put aside—she felt cold and naked, and completely humiliated. Would he die of surprise if she slapped him? She wondered. The temptation to find out was too much for her and she aimed a blow at the side of his face, shutting her eyes in case the result hurt her more than it did him. The contact was brief and feeble and she was unaccountably disappointed that she hadn't been more successful.

'All right, all right,' he said, holding her away from him with an ease that added to her mortification. 'I apologize – though it wasn't all my fault!' His hold on her arms relaxed and a glint of amusement came back into his eyes. 'If you want to hit me, you'll have to learn a better technique than the one you favour at the moment, *amada*! Here, you should make a fist like that and let me walk into it! That way, you stand a chance of stopping me, only – next time – you'd better make it *before* I kiss you rather than afterwards!'

Rachel could have hit him hard then, but he was too far away for her to reach and, no matter how provoking he was, she had no wish to be seen brawling with him in the street. She pushed down the lock and shut the door on her side of

63

the car with an icy dignity which she hoped would make her position quite clear to him, far better than any words would have done.

He strode off ahead of her up the short hill that led to the ticket office and on to the Meswar Palace, the gardens which surrounded the erstwhile royal residence, and the bull-ring which was still sometimes used, usually for the kinder spectacle of one of the travelling shows from the theatres of Madrid. Rachel followed more slowly, the conviction growing on her that, as he had apologized, she ought to apologize to him too.

'Jerónimo—' she began. He paused, waiting for her to catch up with him. 'I'm sorry too,' she said.

'For slapping my face?'

'I was afraid I might hurt you,' she confessed. 'I didn't, did I?'

'Not with your hand,' he answered. His expression softened as he studied her contrite face. 'All right, *niña*, you're forgiven – this time! Will you wait outside while I buy the tickets?' He smiled as she nodded. 'Stay here, then. You might get lost in all these crowds and I may not be disposed to come looking for you!'

Her head came up with a jerk, all thought of repentance completely forgotten. 'I can look after myself!'

The sun was hot in the courtyard and the glare was intense as she turned her attention to the golden building around her. Then, with a start, she thought she saw a familiar figure. She made a dash into the crowd, flinging herself into the astonished man's arms.

'*Duncan!*' she cried out with a whoop of joy. 'Oh, Duncan, you don't know how pleased I am to see you!'

The man unpicked himself from her embrace, his face flushed with embarrassment. 'Rachel? Rachel! Rachel Andrews, whatever are you doing here?'

CHAPTER FIVE

RACHEL had never been so glad to see anyone as she was Duncan Sutherland. He was so commonplace, so delightfully familiar and, if he didn't make her feel particularly feminine, neither did he reduce her to pulp by looking at her in that particular way of Jerónimo's.

'What are you doing in Spain?' she demanded.

'I'm on holiday.' He pulled at the collar of his shirt. 'I had thought of looking you up, as a matter of fact.'

'But I didn't give you our address,' she reminded him.

'No, but—' He broke off as Jerónimo came towards them and put a possessive hand on Rachel's shoulder.

Rachel swung round at once, momentarily irritated by Duncan's lack of *savoir faire*. He looked as if he were quite overcome by the Spaniard and the exaggerated respect with which he stood to attention was another black mark against him as far as she was concerned.

'Jerónimo,' she said too loudly, 'I want you to meet Duncan Sutherland, a friend of ours. Duncan, Señor Jerónimo Parades Lucot, our cousin.'

'Ah yes,' said Jerónimo, 'I have heard about you.' He shook hands with Duncan. 'Rosita has missed having you at her beck and call. Is that why you have come to Spain?'

His easy manner contrasted sharply with Duncan's wary embarrassment. 'Did Rosita tell you about me?'

'She did,' Jerónimo returned affably.

'No, I did,' Rachel claimed at the same moment. 'I mean, Rosita told Jerónimo that you and I had been seeing each other for some time now—'

'But that now you are seeing Rosita,' Jerónimo confirmed. 'We have all heard about her friend Duncan, who dances badly, but who is so much better than any

Spaniard in every other way!'

'But Rosita hasn't *mentioned* him since coming to Spain!' Rachel protested, visibly upset at the way the meeting with Duncan was going.

Jerónimo looked surprised. 'Not to you? My mother complains that she will talk of nothing else but the greater delights of living in England and being escorted to parties by her friend Duncan!'

If Rachel had been Rosita, she would have given in to the temptation to stamp her foot and insist that Duncan was *her* friend, that he always had been, and that he had come to Spain to see *her*, not her sister. It was exactly the way her father had always got his own way with both his beautiful wives, but Rachel was made of sterner stuff and, besides, she was more than a little afraid that Jerónimo would laugh at her and that was something which was not to be borne.

Instead, she put her arm in Duncan's and drew him down the path towards the entrance of the palace, allowing Jerónimo to follow on behind.

'Do you remember the day we went to Hampton Court?' she encouraged Duncan. Really, she thought, did he have to walk so stiffly beside her? Couldn't he bend a little and give the impression that he liked her a little, even if he did like Rosita a whole lot more?

'I remember,' he said dourly. 'You had to rush off in the middle to get to work in time. Rosita and I—'

'It was a lovely day!' Rachel cut him off hastily. 'The sun was shining and we went on the river. Do you remember that?'

Jerónimo exchanged a few words with the man who checked their tickets at the entrance, going through the door first and taking advantage of that brief hiatus while Duncan searched for his ticket in his pocket to make sure that he was standing between Rachel and her reluctant swain.

'Duncan,' Rachel told him, 'is by way of being an amateur historian. He'll be able to tell us all about the Alhambra. He's very good at that sort of thing.'

66

'Then you won't be interested in having this book I bought you,' Jerónimo replied. 'Pity, because the fellow lived here many years ago, actually in the Alhambra, and wrote his tales of the Alhambra while he was here.'

'Washington Irving?' She tried to peep at the cover.

'Duncan will tell you the stories much better,' Jerónimo said distantly.

'Yes, that's true,' Duncan broke in. 'I never read anything that's been published longer than a few years. It's always wrong and invariably dull.'

Rachel opened her mouth to tell him exactly what she thought of that comment, but Jerónimo was before her.

'Rosita would probably agree with you,' he said.

'Yes, she does,' Duncan confirmed, looking smug.

'I thought as much.' Jerónimo turned away, moving forward into the Machuca gallery, which must be one of the most beautiful rooms in the world.

Rachel felt torn in two. 'How do you know what Rosita likes and doesn't like?' she asked Duncan. 'You haven't known her long – only in this last six months when I was busy working. I thought you only went out with her to keep in touch with me?'

Duncan shuffled his feet. 'It was a little more than that. Look, Rachel, Rosita wrote to me, only I can't tell her cousin that because she says he wouldn't understand that an English girl is entitled to have her own friends. But if Rosita hears that I took you round the Alhambra I'd never hear the end of it, and I don't want to get in wrong with her. You do understand, don't you?'

'No,' said Rachel. 'I didn't ask to meet you here. It just happened.'

'Yes, well, I don't think it a very good idea. Why don't you catch up with your cousin and hear it all from him?'

Rachel stared at him, a little astonished that she didn't like him better, and a little shocked by her disappointment in him. He should have looked better beside Jerónimo, much better! Yet all the qualities she had always admired in him had faded into insignificance the moment the Spaniard had appeared. Worse, Rachel was almost sure that Jerónimo thought they had both of them made fools of themselves. She sighed. Why couldn't Duncan have been romantic and clever for once? And why had he to go on about Rosita in front of Jerónimo like that? And Jerónimo had encouraged him!

She wandered across the gallery by herself, admiring the fragile, delicate architecture. The decorations were not made from any rich materials that she could see. Rather were the arches used to filter the light through their span- drels, like lace held up to the sunlight. Marble was used only for some of the columns, the rest was wood, stucco, and tiles, sometimes covered by plasterwork, elaborately carved and decorated with geometric patterns, floral motifs, and the firm, straight writing of the cubic letters that proclaimed the glory of God in various quotations from the Koran.

From the windows, the sun-drenched hills and the glare from the white houses, still presenting a Moorish character in their architecture, made a perfect foil to the exquisite decoration of the interior. By contrast, the gallery seemed cooler, and even the endless tread of the visiting tourists were unable to disturb the calm peace that was as much as part of the building as the walls and floor.

'Where's Rosita's friend?' Jerónimo asked her, when she reluctantly came up beside him.

Rachel made her face a blank. 'He prefers to go round by himself,' she answered. *Damn* Duncan!

Jerónimo held out the book he had bought for her with a sardonic smile. 'Never mind, Duncan Sutherland is not worthy of your mettle. He is not for you.'

Rachel accepted the book, feeling a fraud. 'I like Duncan,' she insisted. 'I always have.'

Jerónimo shrugged. 'You are full of these tepid terms of affection,' he told her. 'You like Duncan; you *like* my grandmother! But you don't *like* me, and you never will! Duncan will never warm your blood—'

Rachel lifted her chin. 'And you will, I suppose?'

'Maybe. At least we both know that it is a possibility between us.' He watched her as she stood with her back to the row of arched windows, making a pretence of looking at the illustrations in the book he had given her. She tried to see where Duncan had got to, but she couldn't see him anywhere. She might have known he would desert her, she thought. 'Thank you – *for the book!*' she said out loud.

'Will you read it?'

'Yes, of course.'

'Then I'm glad I changed my mind and gave it to you after all.' He smiled slowly. 'Your hair is just the colour of the sunlight coming through the spandrels. I have never seen such fair hair before.'

She wasn't expecting the compliment and she said the first thing that came into her head to cover her pleasure at his words. 'When I was a child, I always wanted to be dark and glamorous – like Carmen. I still have hankerings sometimes to be a brunette, especially in Spain. I stand out like a sore thumb here!'

'Don't you wish to stand out?' He looked amused. 'Ah, there is the likeable Duncan again. You will wait for me here, if you please, Raquel, while I have a word with him. Rosita will expect me to ask him to the house, don't you think?'

'Would you ask him if I wanted you to?' She wished she hadn't asked, especially as he took the question seriously, weighing it, and her, up in his mind as he considered his answer.

'Probably not,' he said. 'If he comes, he comes as Rosita's friend and you will not interfere in that—'

'He's my friend too!'

'No, he is not your friend. You would only make it more difficult for your sister, and that I can't allow. Rosita is entitled to have her moments too, *niña*!'

But Rosita didn't care a row of pins about Duncan! Besides, Doña Nicolasa meant to have Rosita for her daughter-in-law and wouldn't relish being expected to entertain any Englishman on her niece's behalf. Rachel wondered if Jerónimo knew of his mother's plans for his marriage. It was hard to know, because he seldom gave anything away. Spanish men were very hard to understand, as Carmen had frequently told her. They thought nothing of flirting with any pretty girl who came their way, often with their own wives looking on, yet they would not tolerate their own women, be they wives or sisters, or merely cousins, to look at any man unless they were married or betrothed to him. Rachel sometimes thought it was all an elaborate Spanish game, for she had seen several wives who were not above trying to make their husbands jealous, almost as if they thought they were unloved and forgotten if they wouldn't rouse their spouses to make them toe the marital line. That the husbands were successful in controlling their wives, Rachel didn't doubt for a moment, but she wasn't nearly so sure that it always worked the other way round.

And she hadn't waited to be married before feeling the first bitter pangs of jealousy herself. She had no right to be envious of her sister, and she wasn't, at least not as far as Duncan was concerned! But when she thought of her married to Jerónimo, all affection died and she was left with a dry, burning feeling of despair that it wasn't she who was half Parades and therefore a fitting mate for him. Could it possibly be that she was falling in love with him? Oh no, that she would not!

But when he came back to her, she couldn't bring herself to look at him – just in case. Her hands shook as she turned another page in the book.

'Is he coming?'

She was rather pleased with the indifferent tone in which she asked the question. She was even more pleased when she saw the faint frown of concern between Jerónimo's eyes. Did he care that she had been pleased to see Duncan?

'Tomorrow evening. I had hoped he could make it another time as Abuela is going home tomorrow and, naturally, I shall be driving her back to Cesares. It means I shan't be home until late, though, and I wanted to be there when he came.' His eyes caught and held hers. 'I shall speak to my mother, of course, and tell her that he is coming, but I should like your assurance that you won't involve yourself with Duncan while he is under my roof?'

Rachel kept a tight rein on her temper. 'I suppose I shall be allowed to speak to him?'

'Of course. I only want to save you the embarrassment of being caught up in something you'll regret and which won't please me at all! So, I have your promise, Raquel?'

Rachel licked her lips, disliking him very much. How could she have been afraid of falling in love with him?

'I don't make promises about things like that.' She looked down quickly, her eyelashes fanning against her cheeks, afraid that he would wring a firm commitment out of her when she had her own plans for Duncan's visit, plans that weren't likely to please Jerónimo at all!

'But you will remember that you have nothing to say to Duncan that can't equally well be said to anyone else?'

Rachel snapped the book shut and began to move out of the gallery. 'What should I have to say to him? Or he to me? Not that it's anything to do with you what I choose to do! Your precious Rosita can look after herself very well without any help from you. If you think I present any competition to her, you must be sillier than I thought! But Duncan is *my* friend. He's just the sort of dull, reliable person that Rosita despises and whom *everybody* thinks makes a suitable boy-friend for me! And I think so too! He's – *muy formal*, and he wouldn't take advantage of anyone!'

The frown deepened between his eyes. 'What stupidity is

71

this now? Are you disappointed because he has chosen Rosita? But a man like him means nothing to you! He has nothing to give you, but boredom and this tepid liking you talk so much about. Such a man would never love you, as you were meant to be loved, Raquel!'

Rachel managed a rather watery smile. 'But I'm a dull sort of person too!'

Jerónimo made a comprehensive gesture with his hands. 'You are many things,' he agreed, 'but dull you are not!' He took the book out of her hand and tucked her hand into his arm. 'If you go looking for compliments, *cara*, you must take the consequences and you can hardly slap my face in front of all these people!'

He was at his most austere when she stole a look at him and her heart-beat quickened with a delicious alarm that she couldn't put a name to. 'But I know all the forgotten corners where nobody goes,' he warned her.

She retrieved her hand and skipped ahead of him into an open courtyard where the hot sun struck her like a blast from a furnace. 'Are you going to show them to me?' she asked.

'Not today,' he returned. He reclaimed her hand and replaced it on his arm, drawing her through another arched doorway into one of the most beautiful little gardens she had ever seen, a fountain playing at either end of a long, oblong pool that was edged about with masses of sweet-smelling flowers. He bent his head until his face was on a level with hers and smiled straight into her eyes. 'How's the War of Independence going, little one?'

Caught unawares, Rachel could only stare at him. She recalled herself with difficulty and uttered a small laugh that was woefully inadequate to the occasion. 'I don't know what you're talking about,' she said.

His derisive smile undermined her last bit of confidence and she took refuge in flight, almost running round the pond to the safety of the dimly lit chamber beyond. Never had she seen such highly ornate decorations as were to be seen there. The domes were covered with carved cedar, inlaid with silver, mother-of-pearl, and ivory, and the walls and floor with tiles faded with age, but no less beautiful because they had lost some of their original gaudiness.

She knew immediately Jerónimo set foot in the shadowed interior, but she affected to ignore him, hurrying through into one of the smaller rooms beyond. Here she was unlucky, because it proved to be a dead end, and she was forced to retrace her steps back to the garden. She stood for a minute in the entrance, lit up by the sun, deliberately turning her back on him.

She felt his hand briefly on her hair, and the pull as he tugged gently on a displaced lock restoring it to its proper place. 'Very pretty!' he commented dryly. 'Do I have your promise now?'

'No, you have not!' she retorted with some asperity.

'But you'll have a care for yourself while I'm not there to protect you?' he insisted. 'Diego will be there. If you need someone to spar with, he'll be delighted to pay you all the pretty compliments you need. But you will leave Duncan alone!'

'While Rosita may do as she pleases?'

His laughter unsettled her, making her feel small for dragging her sister into the argument. 'I think we can safely leave it to Mama to chaperon Rosita.' The wry note in his voice startled her. 'I wish I could say the same for you!'

'But she does,' Rachel felt obliged to point out. 'She doesn't like it at all when I'm alone with you, and much you care about that! She's for ever telling me that I'm not related to you and have no claim on you. She was quite cross that I had been out riding and hadn't told her where I was going first.'

'Is that why you haven't been riding with me since?' he asked.

'More or less. I can't use her mare and her saddle without

her permission, and I don't think she'd give it. And they are *hers*! It isn't the same thing for you to lend them to me, no matter what you say!'

'I see,' he said. 'But you'll come if she tells you herself that you may borrow her saddle?'

'Yes,' she said. 'But please don't make her do anything she doesn't want. Jerónimo, you won't, will you?'

'My mother is tougher than you think,' he remarked.

'Perhaps,' she assented. 'But that's no reason for you to be unkind – and you were unkind to her, you know you were!'

'I haven't your gentle touch.'

She dismissed that with the contempt it deserved. 'Doña Nicolasa is much wiser than either of us.' She hesitated. 'When you come back from taking Abuela to Casares, will you talk seriously about my future?'

'That's my affair,' he bit out.

'Mine too!' she reminded him. 'You mentioned in London that I might find a job in Granada. I can't live on you and your family for ever.'

She couldn't resist looking up at him. He was so very good to look at, with his high cheekbones and the strong line of his jaw. She liked too the way his black eyes contrasted with the golden tan of his skin. She looked away again, disconcerted by the penetrating amusement she discovered in his glance.

'I underrated you, my dear,' he mocked her. 'I see you are busy rallying your forces and are not routed at all. But I fancy my strategy will prove superior in the end.'

'You're better placed to make me fall in with your plan that I should do nothing until I marry and you're rid of me that way, while you support me as Rosita's sister, but I have no mind to be a poor relation and an encumbrance for very long, and I have a great deal of determination, so I think my chances of making you see things my way are better than even.'

74

He raised an eyebrow. 'Ah,' he said, 'but I can call out your fifth column any time I choose, and that rather reduces the odds in my favour, don't you think?'

There was a short, pregnant silence. 'What fifth column?' she asked indignantly.

'Your own feminine nature,' he told her. 'It doesn't come naturally to you to defy someone you would much rather have on your side,' She looked so noticeably dashed that he smiled. 'Admit it, Raquel, you don't intend to win!'

'I must,' she said simply.

'Why? It doesn't hurt you not to have to work for a while. I want you to enjoy your freedom and do all the things that young girls like to do when they have no ties or responsibilities to weigh them down.'

'But can't you see that it isn't right for you to give me so much? I have to stand on my own feet—' She put out a hand to touch the front of his shirt, unconsciously pleading with him to hear her out. 'You may be enjoying playing King Cophetua, but it isn't much fun being the beggarmaid! I want to keep my self-respect.'

He followed her in silence through the next few rooms until they emerged from the King's Salon into the Lions' Courtyard. 'If you were a man, I would allow you to be right,' he said. 'As it is, we have a choice: either you must sacrifice your self-respect, or I mine.'

'But you don't come into it!' she protested.

'I am your nearest male relative. What kind of man would I be to stand aside and permit you to work for a living that cannot possibly compare with what I can provide for you from the family estates?'

'But you're not my relative!'

'Oh, Raquel, what strange ideas you have in that beautiful head of yours! My cousin married your father and that makes me your relation, whether you like it or not. Or do you disclaim Carmen as your stepmother, even if her blood doesn't actually run in your veins?'

75

Rachel blinked. 'I loved Carmen,' she said, 'I miss her very much. More, sometimes, than I miss my father.'

'Then why can't you accept what is your due from her family? It won't be for long, and Rosita would be lost if she had to stay on here alone. Once we have her affairs settled, we can arrange your future to our mutal satisfaction. Isn't that what you'd really like too?'

Rachel perceived that the battle was lost, and knew an overwhelming relief that it should be so. When Rosita was settled, she would have to fight again but, for now, he had provided her with a more than adequate excuse to accept her fate. And a very nice fate it was too, she thought with visible satisfaction. She had taken to her new life like a duck to water and it was going to be a wrench indeed when she had to leave it, as she still thought she must, when Rosita had settled down. Jerónimo's quizzical expression made her wonder if she had given in too easily. She was honest enough to admit that she hadn't liked defying him, though the reason for that was something on which she preferred not to dwell, but she had thought she was right too. Only she wasn't quite so sure now. She hadn't thought that his self-respect might be involved as well as hers!

'You are a wretch,' she said, beginning to smile. 'Soft living has seriously weakened my moral fibre already. It will be your fault if I never want to do a hand's turn again. Oh, Jerónimo, I never thought to be so happy as I am here! I hope Rosita takes a long, long time to get used to her Spanish half! Though I wish she could be as happy as I am!'

'I take it you are resigned to the role of beggarmaid after all?' he said dryly.

'No, because you've persuaded me that I have Carmen to thank for being here, not King Cophetua. It makes a difference—'

'Because you don't have to accept it from me?'

She quailed at the look on his face, but she wasn't going to give another inch. If she did, who knew where it would end?

And it was all the same really. She could save her face by pretending that his largesse was Carmen's gift to her, but she couldn't deceive herself. Doña Nicolasa would have thought the idea laughable, that Rachel was owed anything by the Parades family, and it had been unexpectedly kind of Jerónimo to make believe that she was. She would always be grateful to him for that.

'It's better that way,' she said.

To her surprise he laughed. 'So that you keep your English independence? If it pleases you to think so, why not? But you will need more than your determination to pretend to a man's responsibilities to keep me at arm's length when I decide to end the charade. In Spain, a woman doesn't make her own way in the world when she has a man to do it for her and, when all is said and done, I am a Spaniard, and as fond of our ways as you are of yours.'

'Then you'd better find this Spaniard I am to marry quickly,' she flared up. 'I won't accept the charity of any man but my husband!'

He half-bowed, as foreign as she had ever seen him, and more remote even than when she had first met him.

'I will bear it in mind,' he assured her. 'Have you seen all you want to for now?'

She cast a hasty look round the Lions' courtyard, dismayed that she had let so much beauty pass her by without taking it in.

'No, I haven't,' she snapped.

His face softened. 'There will be other days. You can see it then.'

She stepped over the open drain that ran down the centre of the courtyard, moving closer to the carved lions of the fountain that dominated the middle of the open expanse.

'It won't be the same.' She dangled her hand in the water, pretending to look more closely at the lions. It was hard to believe that they were as old as she thought they must be. They had a modern, stumpy look quite at variance with the

77

delicate decorations of the fretwork that was such a feature of the verandah that ran round the courtyard. 'One can't see something for the first time twice!'

He looked amused. 'Then we must pay greater attention to the remaining rooms to give you a better memory of the Alhambra. We'll save the gardens of the Generalife for when you can give your whole mind to them. They are a breath of perfection and not to be fobbed off as a mere follow-on from here.'

She was immediately afraid that he would find some excuse not to be there when she did see the famous gardens. It wouldn't be the same if he wasn't beside her when she first set eyes on the dancing fountains, the formal flower-beds, and the fabulous views across the city.

'Jerónimo, please don't think me ungrateful because I can't *like* being your pensioner?'

'No, not ungrateful, that is not the word I'd choose. You must make allowances for our Spanish ways, though. In Spain, a woman learns early how to accept gracefully what she must; in England you learn only to compete with your men in the world and it's not enough to be loved for yourselves because you are women. I shall try to learn of you, but you must try to learn from me, *convenido*?'

She accepted his outstretched hand. '*Convenido*,' she confirmed, gravely shaking hands with him.

'Good,' he said. 'It's not so bad, *niña*. There are some things that even God accepts because they are.' He pointed out some writing carved into the rim of the bowl of the fountain. 'This is another poem by Ibn Zamrak. It says that this garden offers a beauty which even Allah did not wish to equal. A beautiful garden and a beautiful woman have much in common. They both bring peace and tranquillity to the man who is fortunate enough to possess them.'

Rachel was silent. To be possessed by Jerónimo was a dream she could never aspire to, but she would remember his words for ever.

He smiled down at her serious face. 'Is that too Spanish an idea for you?' he prompted her.

She shook her head. 'No.' Her solemnity broke into a mischievous smile. 'I was wishing that a handsome man could bring the same tranquillity to a woman, but they must always be thinking they know best, and there's no peace to be found in that!'

ABUELA sat, upright as always, in a carved mahogany chair, watching Rachel as she finished her packing for her.

'Did you enjoy your visit to the Alhambra?' she asked.

'Very much.' Rachel sat back on her heels. 'It's a fantastic place, isn't it? I had a wonderful time! I didn't think it was possible for anything to surpass the Patio de los Leones, but now I'm not sure which bit I liked best.'

'Did Jerónimo point out to you the strange paintings on leather in the Sala de los Reyes? They are in the three alcoves at the back. Did you see them? They are unique in Moslem Spain. Some people think they are the work of a Christian Tuscan because of their resemblance to the paintings in a palace in Florence. I always visit them when I go to the Alhambra and come back with a stiff neck from staring up at them.'

'Yes, I did see them,' Rachel exclaimed, as excited as her grandmother. 'They are let into the ceilings of the alcoves. I wonder how they got there?'

The old lady shrugged. 'No one knows. They provide a strange contrast to the tile dados and the much repeated honeycomb effects and filigree work.' Abuela pursed up her lips in a speculative look. 'How do you like this house, *niña*? Could you live with such a mixture of styles of architecture?'

'I love it here,' Rachel said abruptly. 'Are you sure you only brought *two* suitcases with you, Abuelita?'

'My maid is an excellent packer.'

'She must be! I'm afraid of crushing your dresses.' Rachel turned her head and smiled at the old lady. 'Do you have to go back to Casares tomorrow?'

'I don't like to be away too long. Rafaela – my maid, you

know – likes to leave the front door open all day and then she forgets to lock it at night. I know the *cancela* will keep out the thieves, but I never feel really safe unless I have locked the door myself.'

'The *cancela*?' Rachel asked.

Abuela looked surprised. 'I'd forgotten there are some Spanish words you don't know yet. Haven't you seen those wrought-iron gates inside the front door? They allow the passer-by to admire the patio inside without being able to actually come inside. I like the tourists to see how beautiful a Spanish home can be, but I like my privacy too, so I have a hand-painted leather screen that hides what I don't want them to see. I'm afraid Rafaela might leave it out in the rain when I'm not there to tell her to bring it inside.' She sighed. 'There are so many things to worry about when one is away from home.'

Rachel wondered if the old lady was always so pale. She felt a sharp concern that all was not well, no matter how brave a front Abuela put on before the family. She nodded, pretending that the dress she was folding had her whole attention.

'One doesn't have to pretend not to be tired in one's own home—'

'Raquel!' Abuela stared resentfully at the figure kneeling on the floor. 'How long have you known?'

'I don't *know* anything,' Rachel answered. 'But I thought in the car, when you came to the airport to meet us, that you weren't quite well – that you were in pain. Would you like to tell me about it?'

'No, I would not!'

Rachel waited in silence, adding to the growing pile of folded garments on the floor beside her. The struggle going on inside the old lady could be felt right across the room.

'I'm afraid,' Abuela said at last. 'I have a pain in my chest. Most of the time I can ignore it, but sometimes it is very bad and travels right through my body and down my arms. I have been trying to tell myself that it's indigestion. I eat too much rich food, because I like to eat well, you understand? But it is not indigestion. A little thing like heartburn wouldn't make me so tired I could cry.'

'Have you seen a doctor?' Rachel asked.

'I don't like doctors! I have grown old without them and I shall die before I allow them to poke and prod at my insides. You girls think nothing of showing themselves off. Look at that young sister of yours!'

Rachel got up from the floor and came over to the old lady. 'Darling Abuela, he would have to be a very brave man to take you on! Aren't there any women doctors in Spain?'

'And if there are? What makes you think they would be any good at their job?'

Rachel smiled. 'You're a prejudiced old woman!' she said lovingly. 'Will you see a doctor if I come with you?' She felt the tenseness of the old muscles in Abuela's arm and she blinked, overcome by a rush of affection for her. 'If you won't see a doctor, I'll tell Jerónimo!' she threatened.

'I'll think about it,' the old lady compromised.

'But, Abuelita, the longer you put it off the worse it will be. Please say you'll see someone!'

'I may do. I'm probably making a great fuss about nothing. Now don't look like that, child. It isn't as bad as that. I promise you one thing, if I think it's getting any worse, I shall send for you and you can get in half a dozen doctors for all I care. Old age is bound to bring its trials and, when one has always been the very picture of health, one doesn't take kindly to the slowing down process.'

'On your word of honour as a Parades?' Rachel teased her.

'Get on with you, girl, what difference would that make? Are you going to finish my packing, or shall I send for that stuck-up girl of Nicolasa's?'

Rachel returned to the packing with a laugh. 'Perhaps

82

you'd better! She's weighty enough to sit on the suitcase when I try to shut them. I'm never going to get everything in!'

But in the end she managed to push everything in to the two cases and, between the two of them, they bent the bulging lids and got the edges to meet and the catches to hold. Abuela looked tired and drained when they had finished and Rachel suggested that she should go straight to bed without staying up for the evening meal. The old lady agreed with such alacrity that Rachel felt more concerned than ever about her. Jerónimo ought to know, she told herself, for no one else would be able to make her take care of herself properly. She would listen to Jerónimo.

Rachel caught herself up with a start. Why should Abuela listen to Jerónimo before anyone else? Because he was the head of the household and that was the way she had been brought up? Yet what a relief it would be to cast all her worries on those particular broad shoulders! *He* would get his grandmother to a doctor in a flash, getting his own way about that as he did about anything else. He would expect them all to do his bidding – even Abuela – and she, Rachel, would play her part as willingly as any of the others! How Spanish she was getting, she thought ruefully. A week ago it wouldn't have occurred to her to threaten to tell Jerónimo anything, because it wouldn't have occurred to her that his authority was any greater than her own. Now she knew better. She was beginning to understand what he had meant when he had talked about his responsibilities as the head of the family, when they all looked to him to make their decisions for them. Why, if she stayed much longer, she would be as bad as they were, and how nice that would be! Rachel had had enough of trying to manage on her own during the months after her parents had died not to appreciate the luxury of having Jerónimo behind her now. If that were the Spanish way of doing things, she would be the last to complain!

A great fuss was made of Abuela's departure. The three maids ran hither and thither, fetching her handbag and the selection of articles that she had left behind, perhaps deliberately, to prolong her departure. Doña Nicolasa cried openly, the mascara running down her cheeks, telling anyone who would listen that the pain of the departure was more than human flesh could be expected to endure.

Only Rosita stood aloof from the gaggle of weeping women.

'How can you?' she demanded of Rachel, her eyes full of angry accusation. 'How can you make such a fool of yourself? Anyone would think you were never going to see her again!'

Rachel, slightly surprised to find herself holding Abuela's travelling shawl in her hands, took a hasty step backwards. 'I wish she wasn't going!' she declared.

'Why? You won't miss her. How could you miss any old woman you hardly know? I never thought you'd carry on like this about a virtual stranger—'

'She isn't a stranger!'

Rosita sniffed. 'She is to me!'

Rachel abandoned the argument, taking her place in the line to be warmly hugged and kissed on either cheek. 'Must you go?' she whispered in Abuela's ear.

The old lady sighed, her eyes wet with tears. 'Rafaela gets lonely without me.' Her hands clutched at Rachel's. 'You will come and visit me, won't you, child?'

'As soon as you want me to. Remember your promise, Abuelita!'

Jerónimo strode into the centre of the scene, taking a firm grasp of his grandmother's arm. He came to a stop in front of Rachel, touching her damp cheek with a gentle finger.

'Are you ready, Abuela?' he asked. 'Raquel can see you to the car as she seems to have taken on the duties of your *cuerpa de casa*. If you do invite her to stay with you, Rafaela will be jealous that you have found another willing slave to fetch and carry for you.'

Not best pleased at being call a 'house-body', as the Spaniards call their maids of all work, Rachel helped the old lady into the car and wrapped her shawl round her knees.

'Pay no attention to that one,' the old lady advised her. 'I have only to tell Rafaela that you are my favourite grand-daughter and she will be your willing slave as well!'

Jerónimo gave Rachel an amused look. 'You appear to be learning our Spanish ways very nicely if Abuela thinks you can cope with Rafaela. The rest of the family have always been overcome with awe if she would even speak to them!'

Abuela looked annoyed. 'You make too much of it,' she castigated her grandson. 'Rafaela is – Rafaela! She is capricious in her likes and dislikes, but when she hears about Raquel she will naturally be kind to her. You mustn't frighten the little one with your tales.'

'The English aren't easily frightened!' Rachel put in, tossing her head.

Abuela chuckled, a small, dry sound that was quite at odds with her elegant, aristocratic appearance. 'And like to have the last word,' she murmured, 'no matter how high the cost! *Adios*, Raquel. I shan't forget my promise. *Hasta la vista.*'

Rachel went on waving until the car turned out of sight. Doña Nicolasa, exhausted by her emotions, leaned on her arm, putting one soft little hand over her eyes as though the glare from the sun hurt her.

'Jerónimo didn't say one word to Rosita!' she said suddenly. 'Did you notice that, Rachel? Abuela should have made more of her at such a time!' Her irritation became too much for her. '*You* must speak to the girl. She must put herself forward more, instead of standing around looking as though the end of the world has come. Why must she disapprove of everything we do?'

'She doesn't—'

'But she does! Nothing pleases her! You must find some way of telling her that Jerónimo prefers a little enthusiasm, a little life, not these sulky looks and a lack of interest in anything! Only this morning I told her I had arranged for someone to come to the house to teach her Spanish, and do you know what she said? That she had no intention of learning a single word of Spanish! I have a good mind to speak to Jerónimo about her, but I am so anxious he should like her. I can't bear the thought of Carmen's property going out of the family!'

Rachel sighed. 'I'll talk to her,' she said uneasily.

'You will? Abuela is quite right, you are a good girl, Rachel. Though I think you could have spared us having to receive this English friend of Rosita's this evening. Jerónimo has left instructions that he is to have the best of everything, just as though he were visiting royalty. But *I* have determined that Rosita will not be alone with him for a single minute. I am relying on you to entertain him this evening and to stick with him through thick and thin. You knew him too, didn't you? You must be able to persuade him that Rosita has other interests now, and then he'll turn to you and everything will be all right!'

Rachel began to view the dinner party with increasing disfavour. Her own plans for using Duncan as an unobjectionable escort while she found herself some work in Granada, or, better still, found some way of getting back to England to get away from Jerónimo, had been killed stone dead by Jerónimo himself. He had persuaded her that she had to stay until Rosita showed some sign that her Spanish blood was winning the battle with her homesickness for England, and she had *almost* promised him that she wouldn't get involved in his mother's little plots either. Between the two of them, or all three, if you counted Rosita, her situation seemed less than enviable. She was bound to offend somebody no matter what she did!

As for pleasing herself, Rachel spent the better part of the day resolutely putting out of her mind that Jerónimo's approval could possibly mean more to her than anything else in the world. Given the slightest opportunity, she knew she would fall into a delightful day-dream in which Jerónimo's role as hero was a foregone conclusion. But common sense told her that what she was feeling was no more than a passing physical attraction for a man who was quite unlike any other man she had ever met. It would pass, and she would wonder how she could have been so stupid as to have imagined herself in love with him. She was *not* in love with him! She would not allow herself to be in love with him! But neither could she bring herself quite to give up hope that he might find an English garden very much to his taste – less disciplined, and far less rigid than the neat, geometrical beds that the Spanish favoured, but able to give the same tranquillity and peace, with its softer lines and wide sweeps of green lawn. Would he ever see her that way? Not, she decided, if she monopolized Duncan against his expressed wish and he ever got to hear about it!

For once, Rosita was dressed before her. Rachel thought she had never seen her looking more beautiful. Despite her youth, Rosita had rejected any pleas from her mother that she should wear pastel colours long ago. This evening she had chosen an unrelieved black dress that fitted her closely, and she had done her hair in the Spanish style, adding some flowers behind and just below her left ear in exactly the correct position.

'Well?' she challenged Rachel, pirouetting before her to show off her skirt the better.

'Very nice,' Rachel complimented her. 'And very Spanish. Doña Nicolasa will be pleased.'

Rosita pouted. 'I don't care whether she is or not. *She* doesn't matter! But Duncan has romantic ideas about my being half Spanish. He wouldn't like it at all if I were Spanish, of course, but I'm not, and looking like my mother won't make me so. And the combination of being as English as he is, and looking all dark and smouldering, will be like a dream come true for him.'

'Rosita, how can you say so?' Rachel rebuked her, shocked.

Unabashed, Rosita smiled slowly. 'You never did know Duncan very well,' she remarked. She sat down on the end of Rachel's bed and watched her sister step into her own dress of rose-red watered silk. 'However, it was very clever of you to find him at the Alhambra, so I shan't mind if he pays some attention to you this evening.'

'I was very glad to see him!' Rachel remembered with feeling.

'Only because he doesn't ruffle your feathers,' Rosita pointed out, unperturbed by Rachel's indignant expression in the glass. 'That powder is too light a colour for you. You're acquiring quite a tan out here.'

'It's all I have,' Rachel muttered. She threw her sister a worried glance. 'Rosita, Duncan is a very nice man. Don't play with him because you're a bit bored and not very happy here, will you?'

Rosita stretched and rose languidly to her feet. 'Why not? Duncan and I understand one another. Don't fuss, darling! If you want to worry about something, worry about yourself for a change. Tia Nicolasa wasn't all pleased when Jerónimo said she had to offer you the use of her saddle. She'll make your life hell if you let her. She has other ideas for her dear, darling boy!'

Affronted, Rachel stood up too, abandoning her search for a deeper-hued powder in the drawer of the dressing-table. 'She has nothing to fear from me,' she declared roundly. She swallowed down the consternation her own words had roused within her and went on more calmly, 'Jerónimo wouldn't give me another thought if I weren't your sister. I'm just another tiresome responsibility he has to shoulder because he's Carmen's cousin.'

Rosita yawned. 'I know that! Tia Nicolasa has her eye on me for him because of that hateful *hacienda* of Mama's, but happily Jerónimo hasn't the least intention of obliging her. It's the nicest thing I know about him. One has to admire the way he does exactly as he likes, no matter what anyone says. I'd like to be like that, so it's just as well he doesn't want to marry me. Duncan suits me much better! He's only too willing to do as he's told.'

'Are you *serious* about Duncan?' Rachel asked.

Her sister laughed. 'Poor Rachel, you've never known when I was joking, have you? Well, I'm not telling you! But I will tell you this, I mean to get back to England as fast as I can, and neither you nor Tia Nicolasa is going to stop me!'

Rachel faced the fact that she had no means of controlling her sister and tried to make the best of the situation, telling herself that this time Rosita had certainly been making fun of her as Duncan hadn't an ounce of romance in him and very likely wouldn't notice Rosita's Spanish beauty. Indeed, the whole evening had got out of hand and it hadn't begun yet! If only Jerónimo were there to make everything come out right. *He* would know exactly how to handle Rosita, and his mother wouldn't dare to openly matchmake in his presence, and Rachel herself would have been much more comfortable to have left everything to him and not to have had to worry herself to death that it would all be her fault when everything went wrong – as it surely must, if Duncan made sheeps' eyes at Rosita all evening, and he probably would, because he was not only unromantic but, in her opinion, more than a little stupid as well! Was she suffering from sour grapes? She searched her conscience and found it clear. She didn't give two pins for Duncan and she never had!

She was none the less interested to see him arrive in full evening dress, his white tie showing the tell-tale marks of having been tied with none too clean hands, and his tails sadly creased as he had been unable to find anyone to iron them for him at his hotel.

'I don't suppose you could do it for me now?' he asked Rachel.

A hint of mischief lit her eyes. 'Why don't you ask Rosita?' she countered. 'You're here as her guest, you know.'

'I couldn't do that!' he exclaimed. 'She looks gorgeous in that dress, but it isn't very practical for doing household chores in.'

Whereas hers was, Rachel concluded grimly. 'Well, I'm not going to do it either! You'll have to wear it as it is.'

He went on grumbling all the way through the hall to the *sala* where the rest of the family had already gathered, but the moment he set eyes on Rosita's lovely form he fell silent and it was as much as Rachel could do to make sure she had his attention when she introduced him to Doña Nicolasa.

'*Mucho gueso, señor,*' that lady said in freezing tones.

Duncan's hand went straight to his stiff collar. 'Er – I don't understand Spanish, I'm afraid.' He looked about him, his eyes staring. 'Rosita!' he croaked. 'Rosita, you'll have to translate for me.'

'Me?' said Rosita, looking amused. 'But, Duncan, you know I can't speak a word of anything but English. Rachel is the gifted member of the family. You'll have to ask her!'

Fortunately a diversion was caused by the arrival of Jerónimo's younger brother, Diego, with his young wife on his arm. Diego was exactly as Jerónimo had described him – small and well covered, with a slightly anxious expression on his face. This latter was caused by the fact that Paca, his bride of a few months, had taken the opportunity on the drive over from their house on the other side of the city to tell him that he was shortly to become a father. Far from being overjoyed at the news, he was obsessed with the idea that she should be taken home immediately and put to bed before anything worse happened to her.

When Paca kissed her mother-in-law and whispered her

news to her, Diego stood by in an agony of embarrassment. '*Sinvergüenza!*' he berated her as soon as he had her to herself. 'There are strangers present!'

'But none of them understood,' Rachel comforted him, only realizing afterwards that she, too, might have been bracketed with the others.

Paca laughed delightedly. 'You see,' she said to her husband, 'your cousin thinks you terrible for calling your own wife shameless. Jerónimo told you that Raquel would understand everything you say, but you didn't believe him, and now she has seen what a great big bully you are!' She turned on her heel to say a few words to Rosita in her carefully learned English, and then held out her hand for Duncan to kiss, looking slightly puzzled when he did nothing of the kind, but shook it firmly instead. 'Oh, but I forgot!' she exclaimed. 'The English don't kiss the hands of married ladies. I remember the nuns telling me so.'

'The nuns?' Duncan repeated, looking rather faint.

'But yes,' she said simply. 'I have never been to England, you see, but I went to school at the Irish convent in Seville. There we had to speak English all the time, but, I'm afraid, with an Irish accent! You will have to forgive any mistakes I make, yes?'

'Well, yes,' he agreed. 'The thing is we don't lisp in English, otherwise you speak it rather well.'

'Oh, I see,' said Paca. She exchanged glances with Rachel, trying not to giggle. Rachel's spirits sank still lower. Did Duncan have to be so stuffy? And how could he be so superior when he couldn't speak a word of Paca's language? Paca sat down on an elegant but acutely uncomfortable chaise-longue and patted the velvet cushion beside her. 'Do sit here, Raquel, I have been so wanting to meet you. Jerónimo said you had hair like sunshine and cheeks like the petals of a flower, and now I can see you for myself, I see he is quite right!'

Rachel smiled. 'It's only because blondes are unusual in

Spain. I feel quite insipid beside you and Rosita. And that lovely *mantilla* you're wearing would look nothing on me. Your black hair gives it distinction, I think.'

'*Gracias*. This *mantilla* has been long in my family.' She whipped it off her head and held it out for Rachel to examine more closely. 'It is beautiful, isn't it? But it isn't true, Raquel, what you say about your silver hair. Look, you must try it on and see for yourself.'

She leaned forward and placed the *peineta*, the high tortoiseshell comb that holds the *mantilla* on Rachel's head, draping the thick, lacy folds of the *mantilla* over it, arranging it carefully before fastening it at the back with her own brooch of rubies and pearls in the correct manner. When she had done, she held up the mirror from her handbag, her eyes brimming over with laughing satisfaction. 'Do you like it?' she asked.

Rachel had to admit that it suited her very well. 'It would look lovely on anyone! But I can't wear it!'

'It is yours,' Paca insisted. '*A tu disposición*, Raqual.'

Rachel knew better than to take such largesse at its face value, but after a while she realized that the other girl really meant her to have it. Even Diego was called upon to admire the gift and to add his persuasions to hers.

'Jerónimo will admire it greatly!' Paca whispered. 'It would be a shame to deprive him of the pleasure of seeing you in it. But you must wear it just so, Raquelita. Rosita will fix it for you, as she has an eye for these things. Look how well she is wearing those flowers. Most foreigners put them too high up and the effect is ruined.' She turned to the room in general. 'See how Spanish our little cousin looks now!' she invited them.

Rachel looked shyly about her, convinced that Doña Nicolasa would be far from pleased at the transformation, but it was not she but Rosita who came across the room like a fiery bullet and wrenched the *mantilla* from her sister's head.

'How could you, Rachel?' she stormed. 'You know I wanted to look Spanish this evening! And you're not Spanish at all! You look ridiculous, if you want to know! And don't think I shan't tell them why you want to compete with me all the time! Do you think they don't know that you're jealous because Duncan likes me better than he does you?'

Doña Nicolasa retrieved the *mantilla* from Rosita's angry fingers, returning it with a bleak smile to Paca. 'That is quite enough, Rosita.' Something in the quiet tone of voice froze the young girl to the spot. 'I should be failing Carmen's memory if I were to permit such an ill-mannered display from her daughter in my house. You will go to your room – at once, if you please!'

Rosita's face fell. 'But Duncan came to see me,' she protested.

The older woman permitted herself a brief smile. 'He has seen you, *cara*. We have all seen more than enough!'

Rachel felt so sorry for her crestfallen sister that she turned impulsively to Doña Nicolasa. 'Rosita didn't mean any harm,' she pleaded with her. 'If she were to apologize—'

Jerónimo's mother favoured her with an austere look that was very like her elder son's. 'Rosita has to learn her lesson as I had to learn mine,' she said obliquely. She waited for the younger girl to reluctantly leave the room. 'That reminds me, my dear,' she went on, just as if nothing had happened at all, 'I am told that you would sometimes like to go riding in the early mornings. It will be a pleasure for me to know that my mare is being properly exercised. She is completely broken to the side-saddle, so you need not fear that she will run away with you. I seldom ride these days and will make you a gift of the saddle when Jerónimo says you are good enough to go out by yourself.'

Unable to support herself any longer, Rachel sat down quickly on the nearest chair. 'You're very kind, *señora*,' she said weakly.

'No,' Doña Nicolasa retorted stiffly, 'I am not kind, but I hope I am just. Shall we go in to dinner?' She put her arm on Diego's and allowed him to lead her out of the *sala* into the dining-room.

'Quickly,' whispered Paca. 'I'll put the *mantilla* on for you again. It would be a pity not to wear it now.'

Rachel submitted to her neat hands because she was too exhausted to do anything else. Duncan, too, looked wan and defeated. He came and stood beside her, getting in Paca's way, but standing his ground with the dogged persistence of a schoolboy who doesn't know why he's being punished.

'I agree with Rosita,' he said. 'It doesn't suit you.'

Paca pushed him out of her way without ceremony. 'You think that because you aren't accustomed to seeing her look so distinguished – so elegant! If you always saw her so, you would see how beautiful she is!'

Duncan merely looked uncomfortable. 'I say, Rachel,' he began, 'you must know I haven't any quarrel with you, but I don't think it would be fair to Rosita if I stayed on now. Could you explain to Señora Parades that I thought it better not to stay?'

Rachel looked up at his red face, a little surprised by this show of loyalty towards her sister.

'Rosita may be allowed back later,' she said, more optimistically than she felt. 'Won't you wait and see?'

'You'll miss a very good dinner,' Paca added encouragingly.

'No. Thank you all the same.' He was silent for a moment. 'She said she was unhappy, but I never thought she'd have to put up with anything like this!' He made a last desperate effort to straighten his tie. 'Tell her I have to go back to England, but that I'll think of something. You won't forget, will you, Rachel? I don't want the poor little thing to think that I've deserted her too!'

Torn between a strong desire to tell him that far from being deserted, Rosita was the constant concern of her whole family, and an unexpected admiration that Duncan should feel strongly enough about anything to take a stand, Rachel ended up by saying nothing at all. She watched him leave the room, open-mouthed, already worrying because she didn't feel more guilty at his going.

'Should I go and call him back?' she consulted Paca.

The Spanish girl made an eloquent gesture with her shoulders. 'What good will it do you?' she asked with faultless logic. 'You'll never make Jerónimo jealous with that one, *hija*, so of what use is he to you?'

CHAPTER SEVEN

ROSITA'S sobs could be heard right across the *carmen*, the small walled garden that separated her room from Rachel's. Rachel's conscience smote her. She should have gone in to see her earlier instead of enjoying herself at the dinner table with Diego and Paca. Duncan's going had not been the embarrassment to the others she had feared. On the contrary, they had settled back with a sigh of relief, lapsing comfortably into Spanish, and had included Rachel in the luxury of a pleasant family meal where all the members are fond of one another and nobody has to be careful that they might give offence by anything they might say.

It had been a wonderful meal. For once the plates had been heated and the beautifully fried fish had come straight out of the frying pan and not re-heated from the morning. The fish had been followed by *revoltillos*, a kind of beef olive, that Rachel had not tasted before. As these too were piping hot, she could only think that Doña Nicolasa had insisted on a special effort for the night as unexpected as it was welcome, for Jerónimo's mother was at one with Sebastiana, the cook, in thinking that it was quite natural to eat one's food half cold as long as it was prepared with the exacting standards of cleanliness that prevail in every Spanish kitchen.

Rachel, who had eaten more luscious melons since coming to Spain than she had in her life before, was surprised that they were never served at night.

'But, Raquel,' Paca said, her eyes wide with dismay, 'you must never eat melons at night! In the morning a melon is like gold, at midday like silver, but at night it kills!'

Doña Nicolasa and Diego both nodded assent to this dictum. 'It is well known,' they insisted.

'But I've often eaten melon at night and I'm still alive!' Rachel exclaimed.

Three pairs of eyes had studied her with indulgent superiority. 'In England the melons are confused by travelling and are never very good,' Paca assured her with all the confidence of one who has never been to England and therefore knows all about it, 'but in Spain if you eat melons at night you will suffer from terrible wind in the stomach. If you don't believe me, you must ask Abuela. Melons are her passion, and many a night she has spent sleepless as a consequence!'

As they had sat down to dinner at ten o'clock, it was already after eleven when they had returned to the *sala* to be served their coffee by a highly talkative Sebastiana, who had enjoyed the dinner party more than anyone.

'Señorita Rosita would eat nothing!' she announced. 'The going of the English *señor* upset her, no doubt. She wished me to bring the Señorita Raquel to her, but I decided to leave her to fry in her own oil.' She smiled across the room at Rachel. 'Why should you be disturbed when I had made the *cabello de angel* especially for you?'

Rachel tried to look grateful. The sickly sweet dessert made from the stringy inside of the pumpkin and called for obvious reasons Angel's Hair had never been a favourite of hers, though Rosita had occasionally prevailed on Carmen to make it for her as it had appealed strongly to her sweet tooth as a child.

'Perhaps I should go to her now?' Rachel was reluctant to leave the others and she sounded more wistful than she knew. Besides, at any moment now Jerónimo would be coming home and he would see her in Paca's *mantilla*. It would be a long time, if ever, before she summoned up sufficient courage to wear it again. 'I'll take her a cup of coffee and a few of these little cakes. You don't mind, Doña Nicolasa?'

The older woman gave her consent with a slight smile,

and Paca helped Rachel to put an assortment of sweet-meats on a plate for her sister.

'You must both come over and visit us one day soon,' she invited her. 'Diego will collect you if Jerónimo is too busy to come with you. Rosita may like to see a less formal house-hold, don't you think? Our house is very modern – not a bit like this one.'

Rachel smiled. 'I like this one. It's the most beautiful house I've ever seen.'

Paca made a face. 'Beautiful, yes, but I prefer my labour-saving gadgets. You are welcome to Jerónimo's pomp and majesty!'

Feeling rather shattered by the implications of that remark, Rachel made her exit with a heightened colour and as much dignity as could survive Paca's warm embraces and Diego's more restrained goodnight wishes. Even Doña Nicolasa had signified that she expected Rachel to kiss her smooth, scented cheek instead of the more formal handshake they had exchanged formerly.

'Tell Rosita that we shall say no more about this evening's affair. I expect she is fretting about her behaviour. Poor little thing! You must assure her that it is already forgotten, and that none of us will breathe a word to Jerónimo, so she has nothing more to worry about!'

'What about Duncan?' Rachel couldn't resist asking.

Doña Nicolasa was astonished that she should consider him at all. 'It was a politeness to invite him, no more than that. He will not expect to hear from us again,' she said positively.

Not wishing to antagonize her sister, Rachel went first to her own room to remove the *mantilla* from her hair. It was then that she heard Rosita crying and wished that she had gone to her earlier. It had been such a small thing to have had such devastating results. She should have faced up to Doña Nicolasa herself, she thought, for nobody knew better than she that neither her father nor Carmen had found it in their hearts to rebuke Rosita for her frequent outbursts, and it must have come as a shock to her when her aunt had been so severe with her.

The first time she knocked, Rosita didn't answer. Rachel knocked a second time and turned the handle, opening the door a crack.

'May I come in?'

'I can't stop you!' Rosita muttered, turning her face to the wall.

Rachel sighed. 'I've brought you some coffee and something to eat. Sebastiana said you wouldn't eat anything earlier.'

'*Earlier!* I might have eaten something at a civilized hour, but any appetite I have is always gone by the middle of the night. I *hate* having to eat so late. In fact I hate living in Spain!'

Rachel put the cup of coffee on the bedside table where Rosita could reach it easily and looked round for somewhere to stand the cakes. 'It isn't as bad as all that,' she tried to comfort her. 'You only think so because you're upset.'

Rosita sat up at that, presenting a drowned face that otherwise showed no signs of the storm of weeping she had just passed through. 'Oh, don't be so patronizing! It was all your fault anyway!'

Rachel tried not to feel guilty. 'I couldn't help Paca—'.

'Of course you could! You're so anxious that they should all like you that you won't say boo to any of them. What does it matter if Paca likes you or not?'

'I like her! She's a charming person. Of course I want her to like me too. So would you, if you gave yourself a chance.'

Rosita sipped her coffee, managing to look hurt and upset at the same time. 'It was all your fault! How could you, Rachel? I took the trouble to tell you how susceptible Duncan is to a bit of glamour, and then you had to go and do that to me!'

'But I didn't do anything!'

Rosita sniffed. 'You're not wearing the *mantilla* now. Did Paca take it back again?'

'No. I took it off before I came in here,' Rachel confessed.

'A bit late, wasn't it? After you'd had Duncan sitting opposite you, admiring you, all through dinner.'

Rachel sat down on a stool, wondering where to begin. It was useless talking to Rosita when she was in one of her moods, but she had to tell her about Duncan's gallant gesture – if she would let her.

'He wasn't there at dinner,' she began.

Rosita fiddled with the radio beside her bed and the voice of Teresa Jareño came flooding into the room, singing the flamenco song of *Vienen bajando.*

'Can you believe it? One can't even get any civilized music!' Rosita fumed. 'I suppose you're going to tell me that you like their music too?'

'Yes, I do,' Rachel agreed in a low voice.

Rosita snapped the wireless off again. 'You would!' she said scornfully. 'What do you mean, Duncan wasn't there?'

'He wouldn't stay after – after Doña Nicolasa sent you to your room. It was rather impressive, Rosita, and you're not to laugh at him. He said he quite understood why you were unhappy here, and then he walked out. He told me to tell you he has to go back to England, but that he'll work something out, and you're not to worry.'

'Poor Duncan!' said Rosita.

'Well, I think you may be flattered,' Rachel told her with some asperity. 'He hated doing it. He was all red and awkward, but at least he stood up for you.'

'Yes, poor dear, he hates to put himself in the limelight. Where did he say he was going?'

Rachel absently picked up one of the cakes and started to eat it. 'I told you, he's going back to England.'

'Not in the middle of the night, he isn't. Pay attention, Rachel, instead of stuffing yourself with my supper. Which hotel is he staying at?'

Rachel almost dropped her cake in her agitation. 'I don't know. I never asked him. I don't think anybody knows!'

'Then we haven't much time,' Rosita cried out, sitting up with a bounce. 'You'll have to go in one direction while I go in the other until we find him. I've got to talk to him—'

'Certainly not!' Rachel decided. 'At this time of night?'

'What's that got to do with it? I wouldn't ask you if I didn't think you owed it to me, stealing my thunder like that, when you particularly knew that I wanted to make a terrific impression on Duncan. You spoiled it all for me, as you usually do, so you'll have to come with me now.'

'I won't!'

Rosita paid no attention at all to her sister's disapproval. Calmly, her tears miraculously forgotten, she tore off her nightdress and pulled on the nearest shirt and jeans, zipping up the fastenings with a slight wriggle.

'You'd better go and change,' she advised Rachel. 'I'm not going to wait for you and, as you know jolly well you'll come in the end, you'll never get out of the house without being seen by yourself!'

'What makes you think you will?' Rachel asked faintly.

'You don't suppose I've been sitting around twiddling my thumbs all day ever since we got here?' Rosita answered with contempt. 'Hurry up, Rachel!'

Rachel gave her sister an anxious look. She thought her jeans fitted her far too well, and her shirt not well enough, it was so tight across the bust. Indeed, Rosita had only bothered to do up half the buttons. 'Don't you ever wear any underclothes?' she demanded.

Rosita looked amused. 'Rachel, you are the end! So what? I'm a modern, liberated young lady, and I like to look the part.'

'That's all very well, but you may get more attention than you like if you go around like that. Spanish men aren't at all backward at making the most personal comments!'

'Now I wonder how you know that?' Rosita drawled. 'Oh, do hurry up! I'd leave you behind as you have to flap so much about everything, but I may need someone to talk Spanish and Duncan can't.'

'If Doña Nicolasa finds out—'

'Why should she? Unless you feel bound to tell her tomorrow, and I don't care if you do. It'll be too late then to do me any harm!'

Rachel sat down again on the stool, refusing to move one inch until she found out what was going on in Rosita's mind. 'Rosita, you're not going to do anything rash, are you? Jerónimo will be back soon and he may know where Duncan is. It was he who asked him to dinner.'

'I don't need Jerónimo will be back soon and he may know where Duncan is. It was he who asked him to dinner.'

'I don't need Jerónimo to tell me what to do!'

'Please, Rosita, be sensible. Doña Nicolasa went too far, perhaps—'

'As if I care what that old witch does!' Rosita denied.

'But you did care!' Rachel protested. 'I was there, remember.'

'Well, she shouldn't have mentioned Mama as a kind of moral yardstick for me to live up to. Mama would have understood about Duncan. She would have *helped* me, not whisked me off to Spain without even asking me, shutting me up in this museum of a house, with no one to talk to and nothing to do. She would have thought of something so we could have stayed in England.'

Rachel was hurt. 'I did try to make a go of things by ourselves. But we couldn't have gone on—'

'It wouldn't have been for long! Duncan was coming along nicely even then.'

Rachel froze. 'What do you mean?'

'I mean that he had almost decided to ask me to marry him,' Rosita explained patiently. 'I wanted him to for ages, long before he gave up going out with you. In fact he would probably still be thinking you his ideal girl if I hadn't given him a push in the right direction. Oh, Rachel, you are *maddening*! It's nothing to cry about! You don't even like Duncan – you just think you ought to because he has all the virtues that you've told yourself are the ones you admire. He's kind, and he doesn't ask very much, and he bores you stiff!'

'Doesn't he bore you?' Rachel asked carefully.

'No, you silly thing, he doesn't. It's difficult for me to be bored by anyone who thinks everything I do is absolutely marvellous. I know I have feet of clay, but I have no intention of pointing it out to him. He's much happier thinking that he's caught himself a gorgeous goddess, who actually needs him in some remarkable way, and who'll allow himself to be gently worshipped by him for as long as he likes, without frightening him half to death by making him make all the decisions all the time. I'll make them for him.'

'But you're much too young to get married!' Rachel said weakly. 'You've only just left school!'

'What's that got to do with it?'

Rachel wondered herself. Looking at her sister, she wondered if she had ever really known her at all. Where had the little girl gone? Rosita urged her to her feet and pushed her towards the door. 'I'm *relying* on you, Rachel. Do go and get changed!'

As she took off her long dress, Rachel told herself that she had known all along that the evening was going to be too much for her. If only Jerónimo had been there! She should have left Rosita to cry it all out by herself or, if she couldn't have done that, at the very least she would have stood up to her and refused to take part in this ridiculous night search for Duncan. The very idea of traipsing round the streets of

Granada, going from hotel to hotel and inquiring for him, made her feel cold inside. They couldn't possibly do it! She was beginning to think though that Rosita's determination was far greater than her own and that she would have no say in the matter. She couldn't possibly allow her sister to go on her own.

'Are you ready yet?' Rosita demanded in a piercing whisper from the doorway.

'Almost,' Rachel answered her, hurrying a little as she eased herself into a pair of flat-heeled shoes. 'No, I'm not,' she added. 'Rosita, we can't do it! Have you any idea what these hotels are going to think when we go in looking for Duncan at this hour?'

'What does it matter what they think?'

'But it does matter! They're bound to know the Parades family and that we're staying here. We can't do this to Jerónimo!'

'Oh, for heaven's sake! What has *he* got to do with it?'

Rachel wondered how best to explain. 'I know you think it ridiculous and old-fashioned, but the Spanish are much more correct than we are. They'd be shocked by us going out to look for Duncan by ourselves – and they'd blame Jerónimo for letting us do such a thing!'

'How do they think he can stop us? Besides, everyone knows we're English, and if they don't know that the English don't imprison their women and set watchdogs on them to make sure they behave themselves, it's time they did!'

'I'm not going!' Rachel declared.

'Then I'll go by myself.' Rosita uncoiled herself languidly from her stance of leaning against the door. 'They'll blame Jerónimo much more for *that*! I'm half Parades myself, don't forget!'

If only she knew what she ought to do! Rachel made an indecisive gesture and finished tying up her shoes, her heart like lead within her.

'Why can't we telephone?' she asked suddenly.

Rosita executed a little skip of joy. 'Oh, Rachel, you are brilliant! Now why didn't I think of that? There's a list of the hotels at the back of the guide book you insisted on buying before we left London.' Her face fell. 'Only what excuse are we going to give if anyone finds us in Jerónimo's study? We can't use the other one because Diego and Paca haven't gone home yet, and Tia Nicolasa will hear us and come out to see what we're doing.'

'There's a sign up in the window of the *bodega* at the end of the road saying that the telephone there is for public use,' Rachel suggested. 'I was looking in the window the other day. It has a bar too, so it might still be open. Do you know,' she added, 'that they had all the bottles of Dry Sack sherry dressed up in little sacks? That's what I was looking at.'

'We'll go there!' Rosita hauled her sister through the door, refusing to allow her any more time to finish dressing. 'Come on, Rachel. You can't back out now, because you'll have to do all the talking. Come on!'

The door that led out to the stables had been locked and barred. Rosita signalled to Rachel to stand still and looked cautiously about her, testing the bolts before she attempted to draw them back. Despite being well oiled, they were stiff, and the resounding thud they made as they were opened convinced Rachel that half the house must have been roused by the noise.

'Suppose someone comes and locks us out?' she said in a hushed whisper.

'We'll have found Duncan by then,' Rosita answered, pressing her lips firmly together as she made one last effort and drew back the final bolt.

As if that was the answer to anything, Rachel despaired. He was more likely to think them mad. Nor was he in the least likely to want to have anything to do with them in the middle of the night. He was stuffy enough by day, Rachel thought, remembering how she had tried to taunt him out of the worthy respect he had always treated her to when he had taken her out. At the time she had admired his self-control and had been ashamed of her own lack of restraint. Now, it occurred to her to wonder if he wasn't merely cold-blooded and whether that had been her fault or his own. Perhaps Rosita saw another side to him, but she doubted it. One thing was quite certain though, she would never dare to treat Jerónimo to a similar display because she was quite sure she would get short shrift from him if she did. Yet Jerónimo had only to look at her and she felt more of a woman than she had on any of the few occasions when Duncan had kissed her good night. If only—

Rosita almost yanked her arm out of her shoulder as she hustled her across the courtyard. Rachel heard the mare whinny softly as they went past her stable and was touched she should recognize her.

'Doña Nicolasa says I can go riding in the mornings whenever I wish,' she told Rosita. 'It's kind of her, don't you think?'

'No. Why should you have to ask her permission?'

'Well, it is her saddle – and her mount too,' Rachel pointed out.

'But that isn't what you meant,' Rosita retorted, unerringly putting her finger on the truth of the matter. 'You meant that you think she likes you enough now to let you spend a few minutes alone with Jerónimo. She'll never like you well enough for that. She'll never think you good enough for him!'

'I don't want her to!' Rachel burst out, irritated beyond endurance. 'Surely I can go riding with him without everyone thinking I want to marry him!'

'That's Spain!' Rosita teased her with a flippancy Rachel could very well have done without. 'Never mind, pet. I'll make Duncan take you back to England with us, if you like, and you'll never have to see my dark, handsome cousin ever again!'

Rachel had no answer to that. She didn't want to go back

to England! It had nothing to do with Jerónimo, of course, she wouldn't allow herself to think that, but there were so many, many things she liked about Spain. Indeed, she was beginning to hope that they didn't contact Duncan. She couldn't think that he would be any help to Rosita and, as far as she herself was concerned, it would only be adding disaster to disaster, for Jerónimo would be bound to think that she ought to have prevented Rosita from such an indiscreet piece of folly, let alone involving herself up to her neck in the whole insane venture. She made a last push to dissuade Rosita from going on by reminding her that there was nothing Duncan could do for her.

'You might get him into serious trouble, have you thought of that? Jerónimo is your legal guardian – at least, I think he is and, if he isn't, I must be, and I'm sure he'd think it kidnapping if Duncan took you back to England. Besides, it isn't fair to him, I mean Duncan, because it's most unlikely he's even thought of marrying you!'

'Oh, shut up, Rachel. How you do carry on! You can't possibly know how Duncan feels about me, or how I feel about him, so there!'

Rachel stumbled over a hole in the cobbles, recovered herself with a muttered apology, and promptly took herself to task for being such a craven ninny where her sister was concerned.

'Well, I suppose there's no harm in your talking to him,' she said, trying to sound as though she was in charge and not meekly following Rosita into a quicksand of emotional trauma. 'But you're not going anywhere with him! Now hear me, darling, because I mean what I say. If Jerónimo says you are to stay in Spain—'

'Jerónimo isn't stupid!' her sister declared.

Rachel was rendered speechless. How could Rosita have thought she meant that? Jerónimo was very far from being stupid, but he did expect those around him, especially if they happened to be of the female sex, to do his bidding without question.

'Of course he isn't stupid,' she said aloud, controlling her voice with an effort. 'But you are in his care—'

'Then why do you make out that he would be stupid enough to forbid me to go to England with Duncan?' Rosita retorted. 'If he had wanted to do that, he wouldn't have invited Duncan to dinner, knowing that I had sent for him to come and rescue me from having to stay here a moment longer than I need!'

Rachel felt quite winded by this revelation. 'Do you mean you've discussed marrying Duncan with Jerónimo?' she asked in complete disbelief.

'No, of course not! What I'm saying is that Jerónimo wouldn't care if I did!' Rosita hurried her sister forward, out of the arched gate, round the corner, and into the rather ill-lit street. 'He'll be only too glad to be rid of me!'

'But Doña Nicolasa—'

'Don't listen to her,' Rosita advised simply. 'Jerónimo doesn't haven't you noticed?'

'But, Rosita, she's his *mother*! Of course he listens to her—'

'No, dear, *she* listens to *him*!'

Rachel pushed open the door into the *bodega* and tumbled down the step into the dingy bar. As usual, Rosita had had the last word, but this time she had gone too far. She had to learn that she couldn't criticize those whom she didn't perfectly understand, just because their ways were strange to her, but how to teach her such a lesson was beyond Rachel.

She exchanged a few words with the small, wizened man who came through a bead curtain to see what she wanted. He was more than willing that the two girls should use his telephone. Could he help them obtain the number they wanted? The system was in the process of being improved, but it was not perfect yet.

Rachel showed him the list of hotels they intended to ring

up to find out if Duncan was one of their guests. The Spaniard explored his teeth with the tip of his tongue. Finally he shrugged his shoulders, murmuring to himself under his breath.

'What does he say?' Rosita demanded.

'He doesn't understand why we don't use the phone back at the house,' Rachel translated, feeling cold with fright now that the moment had come when she would have to use the telephone.

'Tell him to mind his own business!' Rosita growled. 'It's nothing to do with him what we do.'

'I told you people would think it *odd*—'

'Oh, Rachel, do get on with it!'

After the first few hotels had denied all knowledge of a Mr. Duncan Sutherland, Rachel should have found it easier to approach the next one. But she didn't. Grasping the receiver more tightly, she waited for someone to answer, and hoping they wouldn't because, quite suddenly, she couldn't think of a single word of Spanish. It had gone from her mind as completely as chalk writing wiped from a blackboard.

'*Ola!* Is a Mr. Duncan Sutherland—?'

'*Si, señorita. Un momento.*'

'It's him!' yelled Rosita, snatching the phone from her. 'Oh, darling Duncan, do hurry up and come!'

Rachel tried to close her mind to the conversation that followed, but she could hardly help hearing Duncan's startled protests that he should have been wakened up at such an hour. Thank God somebody was keeping his head. He would tell Rosita to go home and everything would be all right after all. But Rachel had underrated her sister's powers of persuasion. Duncan's slow answers became less outraged and finally sounded downright conciliatory.

'What have you arranged?' Rachel asked, now expecting the worst, as her sister replaced the receiver.

'I'm meeting him in the morning. We'll buy my ticket

then—'

'*Rosita!*'

But Rosíta was already gone. Rachel pulled a hundred-peseta note out of her pocket and told the man to keep the change. 'The *señorita* is in love?' he asked her with a knowing grin.

Rachel raised her brows in unconscious imitation of Jerónimo and received his hasty apology with considerable hauteur. By the time she had bade them good night and shut the door behind her, Rosita had completely disappeared. Rachel hurried after her, her heart lurching nervously at every shadow, until she gained the arched entrance to the courtyard. 'Rosita?' she whispered.

The door into the house opened, letting out a beam of light. Rachel ran towards it and ran slap into Jerónimo's hard, uncompromising body.

'You're home!' she exclaimed with such relief. 'How was Abuela when you left her? Not too tired, I hope?'

Jerónimo steadied her with a hand on her arm. 'Where is Rosita?'

Rachel hoped she didn't look as guilty as she felt. 'In her room, I should think. Do you want her?'

He drew her inside, looking down at her through narrowed eyes. 'Not in the least. Where have you been, Raquel?'

Rachel uttered a little gasp. 'I took the mare a lump of sugar—' She couldn't tell whether he believed her or not. She tried to look over his shoulder to see if she could see any sign of Rosita, but he was too tall for her to see anything. She had a strong desire to bury her face in his shoulder, which seemed much better placed for that purpose, and tell him the whole dismal story, but fortunately he moved away from her and the opportunity was lost.

'Was she grateful?' he asked her.

'Yes. I think so.'

He favoured her with a long, thoughtful look that made

her ears sing with embarrassment.

'Are you coming riding in the morning? Has Mama told you she is happy for you to borrow her saddle?'

'Yes,' she whispered.

'Then I shall expect you. Good night, Raquel.' He turned on his heel and began to walk away from her, but changed his mind and looked back at her, a faint smile breaking up the sternness of his face. 'By the way,' he said, 'Spanish horses don't eat sugar! We have more respect for their teeth!'

CHAPTER EIGHT

RACHEL was woken the next morning by the gardener watering the plants outside her window. He was singing a *flamenco* song at the top of his voice, oblivious to the fact that others might be sleeping. In a few moments he was joined by Sebastiana, who told him at a shout that she was late getting started that morning and would he please go and fetch the bread for her. The Señora liked it still warm from the oven and would sack her on the spot if she could only produce the stale loaves of yesterday. Besides, if he went to the baker, she, Sebastiana, would give him breakfast in her kitchen. They would have at least half an hour all to themselves before the other maids would disturb them.

This last promise apparently worked the trick, for the buckets clattered to the ground and the voices became quieter and finally went away altogether. Rachel got sleepily out of bed and flung back the shutters to see what the day was like. An early morning mist held back the sunlight, but the promise was good. It was ideal weather for an early morning ride and she felt a little shiver of excitement at the prospect.

Then she remembered. She remembers now why she had lain awake for much of the night feeling progressively more and more guilty, and she knew how important it was to her to prove that the mare would accept a lump of sugar from her hand just as any self-respecting English horse would have done.

Sebastiana showed no sign of surprise when Rachel went into the kitchen and begged a few lumps of sugar from her. She pushed the packet across the table. 'Le convido,' she said. Did the *señorita* require breakfast before she went for her ride, or was the sugar going to be enough for her?

Conscience-stricken, Rachel confessed that the sugar was not for her but that she wanted to give it to the mare to cement her friendship with her.

Sebastiana was openly shocked. 'Sugar is for human beings, not animals!' she disapproved. 'Sit yourself down, *señorita*, and I will make you a cup of chocolate. It is bad for the digestion to start the day on an empty stomach.'

But Rachel couldn't afford the time. She had to get to the stables before Jerónimo because she had to prove to her own satisfaction that the mare would accept a lump of sugar from her hand, if only because it would make her feel better about deliberately lying him.

'*Un bocadillo?*' Sebastiana tried to persuade her. 'A little sandwich?'

'Thank you, no.' Rachel managed a brief smile, grabbed the sugar, and fled.

The mare seemed to have a great many teeth. She lifted up her soft, whiskery lips, and the huge yellow fangs were revealed. But she would not accept the sugar. She obviously had no idea what it was and was more than a little insulted that Rachel should see fit to offer such a strange morsel. She blew down her nose and tossed her head and lifted her soft lips again, making Rachel take a hasty step backwards.

'She's laughing at you,' Jerónimo said, coming up behind her. 'Have you never seen a horse laugh before?'

Rachel lifted her chin. 'Last night—'

'Ah, yes, last night. Where were you last night, Raquel?' He didn't look at her, apparently intent on soothing the mare's ruffled feelings by producing a carrot from his pocket for her delectation. He looked very splendid in his riding clothes – far too handsome for Rachel's comfort. She wished heartily that she hadn't lied to him. She might have known that he would find her out and make her feel as foolish as she was feeling now.

'I can't tell you,' she said obstinately.

He looked round, concerned by the strain in her voice. His

eyes travelled over her, noting the shamed look in her eyes. 'Did you arrange with Duncan Sutherland that you would meet him before he went away last night?'

Rachel was heartily glad to be able to deny that at least. 'Of course not!'

He shrugged his shoulders. 'That is the one thing that would make me very angry with you, *pequeña*. This Duncan is not for you. He is not man enough to be the husband you are looking for. Are you sure he made no arrangement with you?' He paused for her to nod her head. 'Can I believe you – this time?'

Rachel flushed, her eyes falling before his. 'Yes,' she said.

'Very well, I shall ask you no more questions. I am sure you were an unwilling participant in someone else's conspiracy and that you didn't enjoy it very much.' His smile was wintry, but at least it was a smile. 'You must decide on your own loyalties, but I think it would be better for you to give them wholeheartedly into my keeping. You would not find it pleasant to have to make your own way in the world again, would you, Miss Andrews?'

'Is that a threat?' It took courage to stand up to him, but it was imperative that he shouldn't think her afraid of his domineering stance. 'I didn't ask for you to bring me here—'

'But you were not entirely sorry,' he said dryly. 'Confess it, Raquel! Rosita was quite beyond your control and you were worried sick about her. More, your ambitions for yourself are far more likely to be fulfilled in my care than when you were indulging your much vaunted independence in London! It's time you faced up to the fact that you were not made for success in the outside world. You would much prefer to be the centre of some man's home than compete with him for a living by pounding a typewriter in an office!'

'Even girls in Spain go out to work now!' she murmured.

'So they do,' he agreed even more dryly. 'They are not, however, expected to answer to no one but themselves for where and how they live, and the friends they make. They are still part of the family and have a father, or a brother, to look after their interests until they marry and have a husband to take care of them.'

Rachel spent a long moment cudgelling her brains to think of something that would disconcert him and destroy his argument. He was not her father, nor her brother, nor even her cousin, but she thought that would have no sway with him at all. And she was obliged to admit that there was a certain uncomfortable truth in his assessment of her abilities to look after herself. It made her feel very weak-kneed and vulnerable, for surely she ought to want to stand on her own feet, and make her own decisions, as Rosita obviously intended doing.

'You must always be thinking that a woman can't be happy unless she's subservient to some man!' she exclaimed with a quick laugh. 'It isn't true. Rosita isn't like that at all!'

He bent his head towards her. 'But we are not discussing Rosita,' he reminded her, his voice tinged with amusement. 'We are considering your happiness, *amada*, not hers. I am tempted to teach you that you might like it very well to be dependent on a man's good opinion of you and to accept the path in life that he marks out for you. To give your whole allegiance to the man you love is not the small achievement you would have it! It is a perfectly proper ambition in a woman. Why be ashamed of it?'

She was silent for so long that he spread his hands in a gesture of disdain. 'You have no answer? Nevertheless, it is what I shall demand from my own wife. Think well on that, Raquel, and consider if it is too foreign an ideal to appeal to you!'

'I may not marry a Spaniard,' she said. 'In fact I'm beginning to think an Englishman may suit me better. But I am worried about Rosita. She isn't happy here and I don't think she ever will be.' She looked up at him. 'Perhaps you should send us both back to England, Jerónimo?'

'Rosita's happiness is not your worry any longer,' he answered. 'She, too, is my responsibility and I will make sure that all goes well with her. When you wrote to me, you in fact put both your futures in my hand, though possibly that is not what you intended at the time. Can't you trust me to do as I think best for you both? Is it too much to ask that you should trust me to do this?'

'No,' Raquel admitted, her mouth dry. 'I *do* trust you! But Rosita isn't as Spanish as you think—'

'If you trust me at all, you must trust me completely,' he insisted. 'If you want my support, you can't have your own way in everything as well, so which is it to be?'

'Perhaps I didn't manage very well by myself,' she admitted, 'but Rosita is my sister and I have to have a care for her. You must see that?'

He drew himself up. 'You have something to do with Rosita you wish to consult me about?'

'No,' she denied. There was nothing she would have liked better than to tell him that Rosita was going to see Duncan that morning and would probably be back in England by evening unless Rachel did something to stop her. But she couldn't betray Rosita to Jerónimo, no matter what it cost her, and she thought it was going to cost her very dearly. 'No,' she said again.

'But for yourself, you are content to be in my hands?' he pressed her. 'At least until I can find this Spanish husband of your dreams to take care of you for the rest of your life?'

'I'm afraid you'll have to put up with me for a long time in that case,' she retorted, her spirits reviving dramatically as she considered it less and less likely that he would wash his hands of her and leave her to her own resources. 'Do you think you can bear it?'

His smile mocked her. 'I think I can put up with you – in

your proper place!' He touched her cheek with a gentle hand. 'And I'll find some way to make you stay there! You have been warned, *mi pequeña* Raquel!'

All in all, she thought she had escaped very lightly. She watched him saddle up the mare for her, admiring his easy strength and the light way he moved round the horse, making sure the straps were fast and the girth as secure as he could make it.

When he put her in the saddle, she put her hand on his to delay him, her expression serious. 'I'm sorry I can't tell you where I was last night,' she said.

He looked up at her and, meeting the brightness of his eyes, she had a sudden longing that he would hold her tight and never let her go. He lowered his glance to her mouth and she knew he, too, was remembering the kiss they had exchanged at the Alhambra. She turned her face away, unwilling to reveal the wanton way her blood raced at the memory, and how much she would like him to kiss her again.

'I know you'd tell me if it was of any importance,' he smiled at her. 'You say you were not with Duncan and, for the rest, I trust you to behave as I would expect a cousin of mine to behave.' His eyes went to her mouth again, and his smile deepened. 'An English cousin, for most of the Spanish girls I know are afraid to go out in the dark by themselves, starting at every shadow—'

'As I did,' she admitted with a laugh. 'I was scared stiff!' She thought she must have mistaken the glint of admiration in his eyes, but there was no mistaking the constriction of her breathing and the heart-stopping certainty that she wanted none other but himself if he had to search for a Spanish husband for her. But that was foolishness indeed!

'You should make Rosita suffer the consequences of her own actions,' he advised her sardonically. '*She* is not at all afraid of the dark!' He mounted his own gelding, still smiling. 'Nor is she afraid of bringing my disapproval down on her head!'

'Good heavens, no!' she agreed, opening her eyes very wide. 'It must be galling for you to admit that there is one female who doesn't give a fig for anything you say, but there is always Rosita to prove that it isn't our infallible fate to be made to toe the line by you! Think of it – before you know it, Abuela will be kicking up her heels and your mother will be found asking around whether she smacked you too much, or too little, that you never listen to anything she says—'

His roar of laughter cut her off. 'I listen to her often enough when she has something sensible to say! I sometimes listen to Abuela too,' he added on a thoughtful note. 'And I listen to a great deal of nonsense from you!'

He picked up her leading-rein, catching her look of open dislike that he still thought it necessary to control her mount for her, and led the way through the arched gate and out into the road.

Rachel enjoyed her second ride much more than she had her first. She was far less conscious of the distance between herself and the moving ground below, and she was able to relax more, knowing that the mare had no intention of running away with her, much preferring to follow Jerónimo and his gelding at a safe, steady pace. Like all Spanish females, Rachel thought with amusement, she hated exerting herself when there was no imperative need to do so, but once roused she could easily keep pace with the other horse, as she proved when Jerónimo encouraged her into an easy gallop to give Rachel a taste of the joys of riding flat out with the wind in one's face and no traffic to frighten the horses.

When he brought her back to the stables, Rachel demanded how long it would be before she could go out alone.

'Where would you want to go?' he asked her.

'To visit Paca. It would be such fun to turn up on horseback. And she rides too, doesn't she?'

He nodded. 'But not just now. She has never taken to the side-saddle and, now she is expecting a child, Diego refuses to let her ride at all.'

Rachel gave him a surprised look. 'How did you know? She only told Diego yesterday evening!'

'I had a word with Diego before they went home last night and he told me then.'

'And it was you who advised him not to let her ride,' Rachel accused him. 'Don't bother to deny it!'

'It seemed a sensible warning to make,' he responded. 'Diego had no objection to my recommending that she should take things easily for a while. I have a great affection for my sister-in-law and I am fond of children, so I have no wish for her to miscarry if a word from me can prevent it.'

Rachel's eyes kindled. 'I don't know how it is you always put me in the wrong! You know you can't resist having a finger in every pie – even those that are nothing to do with you! I hope Paca appreciates receiving her orders from you through her husband!'

Jerónimo grinned. 'Diego was convinced it was his own idea by the time he left me,' he reassured her. 'And, if he should remember that it came from me, I'm sure he is sensible enough to present it to her as coming from him.'

She considered that for a moment and then said in a rallying tone, 'I've resigned myself to disappointment in hoping that any of your family will ever tell you to mind your own business, but I think it's too bad of you to be always right as well!' She allowed him to lift her down to the ground, her colour heightened by the strong way he held her. She made a play of testing her stiff muscles, grimacing as she walked her first step. 'I do like Paca so much. She was very kind to me last night.'

He kept his hand beneath her elbow as though he were afraid she might fall. 'She would like to be your friend,' he returned. 'She is afraid you may find it lonely here in Spain until you get to know some suitable friends and will want to hurry home to England.'

Rachel shook her head. 'I didn't have many friends in London. I used to go home for the week-ends and that rather limited my opportunities, and then, recently, I was working most of the time and didn't feel much like going out.'

Jerónimo turned her to face him, running a casual finger down her straight, sensible nose, an action which put her into such a flurry that she moved away from him, terrified that he might hear the wild beating of her heart and draw some totally unwarranted conclusions. He, at least, remained perfectly calm, however, lifting his brows in mute mockery as she put up her hands to prevent him from touching her cheek again.

'Paca,' he said kindly, 'knows all the young matrons of Granada and can't wait to introduce you to all her special friends. I'll have to see about getting a small car for your use if you're going to get involved in the social round. Paca doesn't drive and it will be an asset for her too if you can drive her round.'

'But you can't give me a car!' Rachel protested. 'Rosita perhaps, but she hasn't learned to drive yet.' A new thought struck her. 'Can these friends of Paca's speak English?'

'Most of them. Your Spanish is quite good enough for most purposes, though, and it will improve all the time with use—'

'But Rosita doesn't speak one word!'

He shrugged his shoulders. 'So?'

'So?' Rachel repeated crossly. 'How can I go out enjoying myself at – at *your* expense! – knowing that Rosita will either be bored stiff, or stuck at home with nothing to do?'

'Rosita will have other things to do.'

She eyed him suspiciously. 'What things?'

'She will tell you herself when she is ready to do so,' he answered calmly. 'Are you hungry, *pequeña*? Sebastiana has promised she will produce an English breakfast for us. She was concerned that you should refuse her offer of a cup of chocolate earlier.'

Rachel favoured him with a speaking glance. 'Well, I think it was base of her to tell you, but no doubt you make it worth her while to spy for you—'

'*Basta*, Raquel,' he said quite gently. 'She was only worried that you should go out on an empty stomach.'

'She didn't have to tell *you* about it!' Rachel declared, still annoyed.

He looked amused, thus adding fuel to the flame. 'Other people don't find me as unapproachable as you do. My family, my servants, and my friends are constantly telling me things they think I ought to know—'

'I don't think that's anything to boast about!' she interrupted him. 'You should ask yourself why they feel they have to. You ought to be ashamed to have so many people ready to dance to your bidding!'

He laughed. 'Why? There is nothing reprehensible in being well liked!'

'Is *that* why they do it?' she marvelled.

His lack of outrage mocked her, making her feel unexpectedly uncertain. She held her breath, quite unable to tear her eyes away from his.

'Isn't that why *you* are content to put your future in my hands?'

Rachel refused to answer. She swept into the house ahead of him, her stiff limbs forgotten. Nothing would induce her to have breakfast alone with him, tempting though the smell of bacon and eggs was as it came wafting towards her from the kitchen. She went straight to her room and busied herself by washing her hands, ridding herself of the horsey smell that had lingered ever since she had tried to persuade the mare to accept the lumps of sugar.

She was trying to think what to do next and reluctantly facing her own weakness because she knew that in the end she had every intention of meekly going into the dining-room and sitting down opposite Jerónimo, and not even because she was hungry, but because she couldn't bear not to be in his presence whenever the opportunity presented itself, when Rosita knocked on her door.

Rachel eyed her with disfavour. 'You might have waited for me last night,' she said irritably.

Rosita hugged herself thoughtfully. She was wearing one of her prettiest dresses and she was well aware that she was looking particularly lovely and that she had only to coax her sister into looking at her for Rachel's disapproval of her to melt away. 'But, Rachel, you were marvellous! *I* should never have thought of feeding sugar to the horses. And it came out so pat, as though you'd thought it up beforehand. Had you?'

Rachel preferred not to be reminded of the humiliation her lie had brought her. 'No, I hadn't! I think it was mean of you to leave me to carry the can for you! And you owe me a hundred pesetas. I don't see why I should pay for your telephone calls on top of everything else!'

'I'll get it from Duncan,' Rosita promised.

It was much better that she shouldn't know, but Rachel could no more stop herself asking than fly. 'What time are you meeting him?'

'Midday. That'll give us ages because I've already told Sebastiana to tell Tía Nicolasa that I'll be out to lunch.'

'Then you've had breakfast?' Rachel inquired.

'Once, but if you're having some, I don't mind eating it all over again. Ducan may not be able to afford to give me lunch.'

'Good,' said Rachel. 'Then let's hurry. Sebastiana is frying bacon and eggs for us. I could smell it as I came in.'

But when they went past the kitchen, it sounded as though Sebastiana was having strong hysterics. Rachel put her head round the door to see what was the matter and was astonished to see Jerónimo calmly pricking out the pipes of the butane-gas stove, while Sebastiana shrieked that nobody could be expected to fry a piece of bacon unless the flame was hot – hot, and not merely cold – hot as it had been all morning.

'It will be better in a moment,' Jerónimo assured her. 'You must keep these pipes clear to let the gas through.'

Sebastiana denied any responsibility for the state of the pipes or for anything else in the kitchen. What had she found that morning but Concha spring-cleaning *her* kitchen. After such a thing, it would be surprising to her if anything ever worked again.

'I expect Concha was trying to be helpful after your late night last night,' Jerónimo suggested to her.

Sebastiana sniffed, refusing to be mollified. It was her considered opinion that Concha was too flighty to be working in such a house. Did the *señor* know that there were some who doubted the legitimacy of her birth, and yet others who thought she had learned her English from the American soldiers who were billeted in her village and not from her cousin as she had claimed?

Jerónimo bore this information with fortitude, but there was no mistaking his relief when he saw Rachel in the doorway.

'*Menos mal!* Have you come to rescue me? Do something, Raquel, or we shan't get our breakfast until lunchtime!'

Rachel took charge with a will, laughing to herself at his discomfiture. She shut the door after him, straightened her face to an expression of suitable gravity, and turned back to Sebastiana. 'Now what's this all about?' she asked in her very best Spanish. 'Surely nothing is so bad that Señor Jerónimo has to involve himself with the workings of the kitchen?'

Sebastiana stopped screaming and took refuge in a reproachful silence. Rachel ignored her and began to put the stove together again, secretly hoping that she was not going to blow them all up when she lit it.

'Where is Concha now?' she asked Sebastiana.

'Putting on her hat and coat. She is going home.'

Rachel, knowing that the two of them were usually the best of friends, wondered what had happened to cause this flare-up. 'Has anyone told Doña Nicolasa! If Concha isn't going to do her work, she will have to find someone else—'

Sebastiana opened her mouth then all right. Nobody was going to do Concha's work and take her place in the house, or she, too, would go home, and they wouldn't find it easy to find another cook who could cook like an angel and was prepared to produce such exotic meals as the Doña Nicolasa required for such little recompense!

'No indeed!' Rachel agreed promptly. 'Poor Concha is much more easily replaced and she needs the money for her family, doesn't she? Don't you think it would be a kindness, Sebastiana, to go and stop her putting on her hat and coat?'

'And have her spring-clean my kitchen again?'

'I shouldn't think she can do much harm if you supervise her carefully. Is it true that Concha is *no muy honesta*?'

Sebastiana had the grace to look ashamed. 'It may be so, but, *señorita*, if you were to see her dance you would understand why! None can resist her! At the time of *feria* she dances a great deal and it must be that great temptations come her way. It was less than Christian for me to have mentioned such a thing to the *señorito*, though, but he is a good man and will already have forgotten that I did so!'

'I am sure he will if he hears no more about it,' Rachel retorted ruthlessly.

Sebastiana smiled, her ill humour completely forgotten. 'It doesn't do to bottle up one's emotions!' she sighed. 'Please go and seat yourself, *señorita*, and Concha and I will bring your breakfast to you.' She leaned over the stove and lit the gas, blowing on it gently. 'You see,' she exclaimed in triumph, 'at last it is hot-hot!'

Rachel escaped while she could, entering the dining-room with a triumphant air. Jerónimo rose to his feet, a sardonic look in his eyes, and held her chair for her.

'There's no need to ask if everything is peaceful again?' he teased her.

'Of course not!'

Rosita sat slumped in her seat, frowning at them both, 'Rachel is in her element in any domestic dispute,' she muttered. 'She hates people quarrelling all round her, and she always has the answer to the difficulty. Mama used to say she'd make a very good housekeeper one day.'

Rachel felt her triumph slipping away and did her best to hide the hurt look in her eyes. 'Oh, I'm quite efficient *in my place*!' she said airily.

Jerónimo's expression was as austere as ever. 'I never doubted it,' he drawled. He turned to Rosita, his face softening. 'Did you enjoy Duncan's visit last night?' he asked her.

Rosita flung him a venomous glance, but was prevented from answering by one of the maids bringing in the plates and a dish of sizzling bacon and *flamenco* eggs, fried and mixed with tomatoes and onions, with a small piece of anchovy on the top.

'Ugh! *Garlic!*' Rosita complained.

'But it gives extra flavour to the dish,' Jerónimo explained, anxious that it should find favour with her.

'I hate garlic!' Rosita insisted. 'It doesn't agree with me.' She pushed the dish nearer to Rachel. 'You can have mine, if you like?'

Jerónimo and Rachel exchanged glances, neither of them willing to offend Sebastiana any further by sending so much as a crumb back to the kitchen. They struggled manfully through the extra rations, while Rosita nibbled a piece of bacon and buttered herself a slice of bread, preparing herself to tell Jerónimo how badly she had been treated the previous evening. Rachel tried to catch her eye, failed, and ground some pepper over her eggs, sneezing as she did so.

'Jesús!' Jerónimo blessed her.

She sneezed again.

'Jesús – Maria!'

Rosita drew herself up. 'Tia Nicolasa—' she began, and stopped as the door was flung open and Jerónimo's mother came in, seating herself with a flourish next to her son and wishing them all good morning.

'Rosita, *cara*,' she addressed her niece, 'what is this Sebastiana tells me about your going out to lunch? I am afraid it is not possible. I have arranged for your Spanish teacher to come this day, at midday, to give you your first lesson, and you must be here for that. *Insisto en ello!* I insist on it!'

'But, Tia Nicolasa, I have to go out. I don't want to learn Spanish anyway! Rachel will have to see him for me.'

'Him?' Dona Nicolasa was disconcerted for a moment. 'But, naturally, I found a woman to teach you Spanish – so much more suitable in every way! I am sorry, Rosita, if you don't like it, but learn Spanish you must. I didn't want to mention yesterday's fracas again, but I think you owe it to us all to make some kind of amends. Learning a few words of Spanish will do very well.'

Rosita flushed and turned impulsively to Jerónimo. '*You* tell her!' she insisted. 'Tell her that I have to go out!'

Jerónimo stood up. 'As I don't know where you're going—'

'Oh, I hate you all!' Rosita said passionately. '*I hate you!* Well, if I can't go myself, Rachel will have to go for me!'

'Oh no, *please*, Rosita!' Rachel looked round hopefully for Jerónimo's support, but she was too late, he had already left the room.

CHAPTER NINE

DOÑA NICOLASA remained adamant. 'You are being ridiculous, Rosita. Your Spanish teacher is coming and that is that. Nor should you suppose that I would allow you to go running round Granada all on your own, just because you have taken it into your head to see this friend of yours!'

'I'm not a prisoner—'

Doña Nicolasa sighed. 'You are too young to know what you are, my dear. It's not becoming in you to argue with every plan that is made for you.'

'Jerónimo understands!' Rosita claimed, beginning to cry.

'Jerónimo has put you in my care,' her aunt reminded her. 'Really, Rosita, we cannot have these storms and incidents day by day. Your sister doesn't see fit to question our way of life at every turn. Why should you?'

'Oh, Rachel! Rachel is in her seventh heaven! She doesn't *want* to do any of the things you consider to be so terrible! She's never smoked a cigarette in her life, so why should she start now when she knows you wouldn't like it? But I want to smoke occasionally. I want to go to cafés and bars by myself. I always did in England, so why shouldn't I here? Rachel was always as bad as Mama and *she* wouldn't even go into a pub unless Daddy was with her! And I'm sure Rachel agrees with you that bikinis aren't quite nice, whereas I don't have a one-piece swim-suit and wouldn't be seen dead in it if I had! I *hate* Spain! And I mean to see Duncan today, no matter what any of you say!'

'Not this morning you won't!' Doña Nicolasa decreed grimly.

'Why not?' Rosita looked considerably less certain of herself, but she had no intention of giving way. 'Rachel can go and talk to Duncan while I have my lesson and then I'll join them. You can't object to my going if Rachel is there to chaperon me, can you?'

'And who will accompany Rachel to this tryst of yours?' Doña Nicolasa inquired.

'Oh, good heavens, surely you can trust *Rachel* to walk down the road by herself? *She* won't disgrace your precious family name!'

'That is not the point. Rachel is not a Parades and what she does cannot redound on us. But she is a young girl in my care and as such I do not care to have her meeting young men in public places either. What do I know about this Duncan Sutherland? If you wish to have anything to do with him, and this goes for both of you, you must invite him here and let him account for himself to me.'

Rachel was more than relieved by this edict. It would have been hard to refuse point blank to do as Rosita wanted, and yet she knew it would be quite beyond her to explain her actions to Jerónimo. And that was one thing she was quite clear about. He did not wish her to see Duncan on her own, though why not, she couldn't imagine. But she had already gone as far as she dared in jeopardizing his good opinion of her, and not even Rosita's tearful face could tempt her to fall foul of him again.

She was even more relieved when the telephone bell rang. Doña Nicolasa went out into the hall to answer it.

'Rachel, it's for you! Come quickly, child—'

'But who is it?' Rachel approached the telephone with a hollow feeling in the pit of her stomach. 'I don't know anyone here!'

'You know Paca,' Doña Nicolasa said dryly, not best pleased that her daughter-in-law had wanted to speak to someone other than herself. 'I'm going to my room,' she added in an aside. 'Your sister would exhaust a saint!'

Rachel took the receiver from her and held it to her ear.

'Raquel, *olà*! Are you busy?'

'No, no, not at all.'

'Good, because I particularly want to talk to you. I am going to the hairdresser in a few moments, why don't you come too?'

'To me? But, Paca, I can't! I haven't an appointment and—'

'There is no need to book. Nobody does! It wouldn't work if they did. Who would remember to go at the right time? It's a barbaric practice to make up your mind days before that you want to have your hair done at such and such a time!'

'Yes, but what do you want to talk to me about?' Rachel protested feebly.

'That would be telling!' Paca giggled. 'I have that right, no? Now, the best *peluquera* is by the cathedral. If I meet you at the Capilla Real I can take you on there at once and we can talk in peace. Shall we say in an hour's time?'

'Yes, but—'

'That's settled, then,' Paca broke in firmly. 'I had hoped to have Fabiola, my very best friend, with me, for, of course, she is dying to meet you, but she has trouble at home today and couldn't come.'

'Trouble?' Rachel repeated. She couldn't help thinking that anyone else's troubles would pale into insignificance compared to Rosita's woebegone face as her sister came drooping into the hall and stood beside her.

Paca giggled again. 'Her little boy lost a tooth in the night and he expected the little Ratoncito Perez to take it away and leave him some money, but Fabiola didn't know he'd lost it and now she's afraid he'll never believe in anything again! You know about Ratoncito Perez? He is a small mouse and, naturally, he is very popular with children. You have him too in England?'

'In England it's the fairies who buy teeth.'

Rosita touched her forehead significantly, sure that her sister had gone mad. '*She* can go with you to meet Duncan,' she said in a fierce whisper, intent on her own troubles.

'But she might not want to!' Rachel whispered back.

'To do what?' Paca demanded. 'What do I not wish to do?'

'Rosita has a Spanish lesson and she wants me to – to do something for her, only it's all so difficult!'

'But why should I wish to disoblige the little one?' Paca came back in ringing tones. 'By all means let's do as she asks.'

'There you are!' Rosita triumphed. 'You've got no excuse for not going to meet Duncan now, Rachel. You have to go for me!'

Rachel managed a somewhat hurried good-bye to Paca and then faced her sister with a sinking heart. 'I'm not going to promise anything,' she compromised. 'Nor am I going to make Paca do anything she doesn't want to—'

'But she does want to!'

'She may not when she hears who it is we're going to meet! Rosita, wouldn't it be better to ask him to the house?'

'You don't understand! He's going back to England – and I'm going with him! You have to go and meet him for me, Rachel, you just have to! You don't think I want it that way, do you? Well, I don't! But see that you remember that Duncan is mine and that any yen he had for you is *over*! I'll never forgive you if you do anything to put him off me – not that I think you can – but just see that you don't!'

Rachel went to her room to change feeling like a damp rag. Her sympathy for Doña Nicolasa was growing by the minute. She felt more than a little harassed herself. However, she couldn't help feeling quite excited at having been asked out by Paca so soon after having met her. To celebrate, she put on one of her prettiest dresses and went to the trouble of cleaning the straps of her light sandals, knowing that Spaniards set great store by the shine on their shoes.

As she was going out, she met Jerónimo coming in.

'Coward!' she taunted him.

'Not at all,' he returned. 'Acting as peacemaker is your province. Where are you going? Perhaps I can give you a lift?'

She told him about her rendezvous with Paca, pleased to be able to do so.

'Quite a triumph for you,' he congratulated her with a lift to one eyebrow. 'I am glad you refused to act as messenger for your sister.'

Rachel's conscience smote her. 'Doña Nicolasa didn't think it suitable for me to go on my own,' she said primly.

'Very proper. I knew I might rely on her to forbid it, and that would help stiffen your resolution as my wishes never could!'

Rachel looked up at him, threading her fingers together to keep them still. 'Rosita is very stubborn. Your mother's refusal to allow her to meet Duncan this morning will only make her think of something else instead. I thought I ought to tell you that so that you'll understand—' Her voice faded away as she found herself unable to finish the sentence. She knew without his telling her that he was not going to understand why she was not only going to see Duncan herself, but had succeeded in involving Paca too in Rosita's harebrained schemes.

He put a finger under her chin and lifted her face to make sure he had her whole attention. 'Raquel, I wish you wouldn't fret over your sister like this. Won't you leave it to me to bring her round to a more sensible way of behaving?'

'How can I when you walk out—?' His finger on her lips cut off her sentence. 'She won't wait!' she burst out.

'She'll wait!' he retorted. 'This time, *pequeña*, your sister can wait on you, and be pleased to do it.' He released her abruptly and pushed open the front door. 'Wait in the car, will you? I'll be with you in a minute.'

By the time he came out to the car, Rachel had determined to put aside her bewildered reaction to his last words. She must have misunderstood him, she told herself, and really it was not surprising as she became quite hen-witted whenever she was close to him. She had never known what it was before to have her whole being leap with delight at someone's touch. Nor had she experienced the depth of longing that he roused in her without even trying. If he had reciprocated her feelings, how lovely it would have been! But she had constantly to remember that she was only Rosita's half-sister, another responsibility he had acquired along with Carmen's daughter, and that the sooner he was rid of her to the Spanish husband he had teased her with, the better he would be pleased!

'There,' he said, getting into the car, 'you have nothing more to worry about. Rosita has dried her tears and has half forgotten what all the fuss was about. In a month or so we shall invite Duncan Sutherland to visit us and she can see how she feels about him then.'

'Will Duncan come?'

'He will if he is fond of her. It won't be convenient to have him to stay before then, so we will have to hope that he is more inclined to be faithful to her than he was to you!'

'He was no more than a friend to me,' she said in a stifled tone.

'But you didn't always think that,' he reminded her. 'He must have given you some cause to make you feel romantic about him.' He gave her a sardonic smile. 'Is it so incomprehensible that you should have felt that way about him?'

'I think he always preferred Rosita,' she sighed.

'But of course, she is much less demanding than you are. The man who loves you must have fire in his blood and not let you squander yourself on frippery concerns that are less than your total destiny!'

Nettled, Rachel made a small moue of protest. 'I suppose you have my destiny all marked out for me?' She tried to ignore the ache in her heart that her own question had exacerbated. She wanted no other destiny but him!

'I have someone in mind for you,' he agreed.

'Well, I'm sorry to disappoint you, but I don't want to have anything to do with him! When I marry, I want to go to my husband with a whole heart, not marry him because you've picked him out for me!'

He put his hand on hers for an instant before putting it back on the wheel. 'You will love him with your whole heart, I promise you that! Haven't I said he will command your allegiance before all others? You will not have to make do with a few cold kisses from Duncan Sutherland then!'

So Jerónimo thought Duncan was cold-blooded too! 'Duncan Sutherland isn't the only man I knew in England!' she said sulkily.

'All the more reason for you to marry someone who'll insist on having all your thoughts and kisses for himself! You have wasted enough time on those you can only like, now you must accept the challenge of making an alliance with one who will love you and cherish you, but who is man enough to make you his own.'

Rachel closed her eyes, refusing to indulge herself by thinking how wonderful that would be if only he were talking about himself.

'You kissed me too – once,' she reminded him.

'Twice, *amada*.' He looked sideways at her, mocking her, and it was she who looked away.

'I suppose that was different—' she began.

'I regret nothing that has taken place between us,' he cut her off arrogantly. 'Nor, I think, do you. It was, as you say, different, and I will not allow you to say anything to cheapen it because you don't like my telling you that your independent days are over and done with. There will never be equality between us, Raquel, and you wouldn't like it if there were!'

She was effectively silenced. She tried to take an interest

in the streets they were passing through, but she could think of nothing but this husband whom Jerónimo had said he had found for her. How could he think she would accept anyone he produced for her? How could he? The tears burned at the back of her eyes.

'Paca is meeting me at the Capilla Real,' she told him. 'Will you put me down there?'

He stopped the car and leaned across her to open her door for her. 'Would you kiss this Duncan Sutherland now?' he bit out angrily. 'Would you, Raquel?'

She shook her head, hurrying out of the car as fast as she could go. 'It wasn't like that! Duncan never – It never meant anything when he did kiss me! I didn't like it much, if you must know!'

Jerónimo's temper died as quickly as it had been aroused. '*Claro que no*, you were never his, so why should you? Enjoy yourself with Paca, *niña*. I'll see you this evening.'

Paca was impressed that Jerónimo should have brought Rachel down town himself. 'He wouldn't do that for anyone else!' she teased her. 'He would say he had to work, or have some other excuse. You ask my mother-in-law!'

'He was coming this way,' Rachel explained.

'Is that why he turned round and went home again?'

'Oh, Paca! He *said* he was coming this way!'

But Paca only laughed. 'How pretty your hair is!' she exclaimed. 'Do many people in England have such very fair hair?'

Rachel shook her head. 'No, we're a polyglot lot and getting darker all the time. I don't know why I turned out tow-headed. I don't really remember what my mother looked like, but I think she must have been an ash-blonde too.'

'My hairdresser will rave over you,' Paca said generously, 'and all her customers will be green with envy, because she never has much to say, you know, in the ordinary way and we all long for her approval.'

134

Señorita Maruja was every bit as taciturn as Paca had suggested, but her eyes sparkled when she caught sight of Rachel. 'Ah, we have an angel come to visit us this morning!' she declared. 'Sit down, *señora*, and let me see what is the best thing to do for you.' She turned Rachel's head this way and that. 'Ah, *señora*, it is best left as it is.' She summoned one of her assistants with an imperious flick of her wrist. '*Lavar y marcar*,' she commanded. 'The girl will wash your hair, *señora*, but I shall return myself to set it for you.' With which promise, she turned with a businesslike air to Paca and began to discuss with her whether she should trim the edges of her long black hair, or leave it to next time as Paca was suggesting to her.

When, at last, Señorita Maruja was satisfied that she had done her best for her new client and had snipped away to her heart's content at Paca's ends, she left them sipping a cup of coffee while she heated up two driers for them.

'I didn't think before,' Rachel said, 'but I hope this isn't going to be too expensive?'

'But you're my guest!' Paca protested. 'You're not to give it another thought.' She settled herself more comfortably in her chair, her eyes dancing. 'Now, tell me all about this errand we are to do for little Rosita. Did I detect from what you said that you hoped I would refuse to go with you?'

'Not exactly—'

'But you don't approve of Rosita's romance? It seems to me an admirable solution to all your problems. What are we to do? Post a letter for her?'

'Oh, no! It's much worse than that. I can post a letter by myself, but I don't know what to do about *this*. Rosita is determined to go back to England with Duncan – just like that! And, worse still, she expects me to meet him and tell him to buy her ticket.'

'That, *niña*, you cannot agree to do,' Paca decided for her. 'Jerónimo would not like it.'

'I don't like it much myself. But Rosita won't listen to me, and she certainly won't listen to Jerónimo, so what am I to do?'

Paca looked guilty, but she refused to change her mind. 'It would be best to forget all about it. There is nothing you can do, but it is not so bad after all. We will have a lovely morning together and, this afternoon, perhaps Fabiola will join us for a visit to the Generalife gardens. I will telephone her at lunchtime.'

But Rachel refused to be comforted. 'I can't leave Duncan sitting there – not knowing that Rosita can't meet him as she promised. If he went back to England without a word to her, I'd never forgive myself. She wants to *marry* him!'

Paca shrugged her shoulders. 'He is a man, though how she should want such a man I do not know? But he is a friend of yours too, no? I am sure he is very charming when one gets to know him well.'

'Yes, he is,' Rachel insisted with a marked lack of conviction.

Paca looked at her with some amusement. 'Did you think so before you met Jerónimo? But now you can see that there is no comparison? How lucky that you should be Rosita's half-sister!'

'Jerónimo – *all* Carmen's family – have been very kind,' Rachel agreed stiffly.

'Of course,' Paca murmured. Her eyes filled with laughter. 'If I weren't besotted with Diego, I'd hate you, Raquel. The *mamás* of Granada are already sharpening their knives, I can tell you. They were far from pleased to hear of your arrival. Jerónimo is a great favourite with women of all ages. They are all at his feet. He is *muy hombre*, don't you think? And he always knows exactly what one should do. Even Diego does as he says!'

Rachel lifted her chin. 'He's certainly very bossy!'

'You find him so?' Paca looked at her curiously. 'It is much more comfortable to have a man to tell one what to do

136

in the last resort. I admire you so much for trying to manage on your own, for yourself and Rosita, but it's much better now you have Jerónimo to look after you.'

'Yes,' Rachel admitted, 'in a way. But I can't allow him to take me over entirely. He may be related to Rosita, but I haven't any call on him at all. And I have to do what I think is right, no matter what he says!'

'Like seeing this Duncan?'

Rachel nodded unhappily. 'Will you come with me? He'll be waiting in a café, the one on the hill going up to the Alhambra, and even with all the tourists there I don't like sitting at a table by myself. I try to pretend that I can't understand what the men are saying—'

'But they are so clever! Fabiola had the most marvellous *piropo* the other day. He said her feet were so small and neat she could make a Persian carpet with them!' She looked down at her own feet regretfully. 'I'm afraid I'm too clumsy for anyone to say such a thing to me.'

'Will you come with me, Paca?'

The Spanish girl refused to meet Rachel's eyes. 'No, you must excuse me, but Diego would forbid it.'

'But why?' Rachel cried out.

'I didn't want to tell you, but Jerónimo telephoned me this morning and asked me to invite you out to spend the morning with me. He was afraid Rosita would talk you into doing something foolish. Please, Raquel, listen to me! Jerónimo will deal with it all and it is much better that he should. This business between Rosita and Duncan is nothing to do with you. It is not at all wise of you to interfere when Jerónimo has told you not to. Me, I would think twice before I risked his affection for me by making him as angry as he will be when he finds you have disobeyed him.'

'But Rosita is my business! She's my sister. And Jerónimo has no authority over me, none at all! Good heavens, I'm twenty-four, not a schoolgirl!' Her rage gave way to the hurt Paca had dealt her and she went on to ask, 'Wouldn't you have asked me if Jerónimo hadn't asked you too?'

'Oh, Raquel, of course! I had it in mind to do so, but then Fabiola had little Tómas in floods of tears because he had no money for his tooth, and I wanted you to meet her because she is the nicest of my friends and it will be such fun having you in Granada too. You can ask Diego if you don't believe me. I talked of nothing else the whole way home last night – not even about the baby!'

Rachel couldn't help laughing a little at that. 'I see I can't ask you to come with me,' she said. 'I'll go on my own.' She put a determinedly bright expression on her face. 'Who knows, I may receive a really fine *piropo* of my own!'

Paca gave up the attempt to argue with her out of going, but she became increasingly restless under the drier, turning the switch on and off, as though at any moment she would jump up and make some further protest as to how foolish Rachel was being. But when they had both been taken out of the driers and Señorita Maruja had combed out their hair and had pronounced herself willing to see them depart, Paca said nothing more, contenting herself with a quick embrace and a kiss on either cheek.

'*Mucha suerte!* Good luck!' she whispered, and was gone without another word.

It seemed a very long walk from the Plaza de la Lonja to the foot of the Alhambra. Rachel felt hot and tired by the time she had dragged herself up the hill to the café, looking at her watch every few seconds in case she was going to be late. The traffic was thick, going up and down the hill. The hissing sound of the air-brakes of the large coaches vied with the grinding progress of the tiny Seat as they shot up the incline in low gear. Rachel dodged back and forth on to the inadequate pavement, wishing she had taken a taxi despite the low state of her finances. Perhaps Duncan would have paid for it for her?

But Duncan was not there when she arrived at the café.

She took a seat at one of the few vacant tables close to the road and searched through her handbag to give herself something to do, in the half-hearted hope that she might have put the paperback she was reading inside before she had come out. If she kept busy, she thought, she wouldn't be so nervous and, with any luck at all, it would keep the men at bay and they wouldn't think it worth their while to try and chat her up.

It was a quarter past twelve before Duncan arrived. By that time Rachel was desperate. 'You might have taken the trouble to be on time!' she greeted him. 'Supposing it had been Rosita waiting here for you? Anything might have happened to her!'

'Not to her, and you know it,' Duncan replied, throwing himself into the chair opposite her. 'Anyway, why isn't she here?' He shaded his eyes from the sun and looked at Rachel's cross face. 'She still has you on a string, hasn't she? You ought to stand up for yourself more. You look really lovely this morning. It's done you good not to have to work for a while. I kept telling you it wasn't doing you any good.' He wrinkled up his nose appreciatively. 'You've done something to your hair. I like it. I was a fool to let you go, wasn't I?'

'You never had me,' Rachel said. She opened and shut the fastening of her handbag, looking down at it with a fierce concentration. Was it possible that Duncan was as susceptible as Rosita had hinted?

'I might have done if you hadn't always been running off to yet another job. All work and no play made Jill a very dull girl, but you've changed. You don't look as if you could hurry anywhere right now!'

'No,' Rachel agreed bitterly. 'I'm hot, and I'm thirsty, and I didn't want to come in the first place—'

'Then why did you?'

'Rosita has a Spanish lesson.'

'Is that all? Well, I'm not complaining. You'll have to

order the drinks, though. No one understands a word I say to them. What made Rosita throw that scene last night? She looked as foreign as any of them – rather marvellous, but not quite what I would expect from her.'

'That's what she wants to see you about,' Rachel told him, wishing he would summon the waiter or at least look as though he wanted something to drink. 'She isn't happy here in Spain. She wants to go back to England. In fact,' she added, 'she wants to go back with me.'

'And what does her Spanish family say to that?'

Rachel turned round in her seat to stare at a passing waiter and then, when she was almost sure that he was going to ignore her, she clapped her hands and hissed through her teeth at him, trying not to notice Duncan's horrified expression.

'I say,' he said, 'is that the *only* way you can get the man's attention?'

'So it would seem. You may have loitered all the way here, but I was afraid of keeping you waiting and I practically ran up that hill, and if I don't have something to drink soon, I shall expire where I sit!'

Duncan blinked and refused to have anything to do with the waiter when he did come, pointedly looking the other way. When Rachel had ordered a lager for him and a lemonade for herself, he tried another tack. 'Have you just had your hair done?'

'Paca took me to her hairdresser.'

'You, but not Rosita?' He gave her a dissatisfied look. 'Can't you include Rosita in your doings a bit? Her cousin doesn't seem a bad fellow. He sounded quite happy that she should come to England sooner or later, but I can hardly rush her off tonight with me, can I?'

Rachel's eyes widened and she looked at him accusingly. 'Duncan, have you spoken to Jerónimo? Why were you so late getting here?'

'I didn't think either of you'd come,' he answered,

shuffling his feet in the dust.

'*Did Jerónimo tell you that?*'

'Not exactly. Look, Rachel, you'll have to speak to Rosita. I'll be able to take another week's holiday in a couple of months and I'll come and see how she's getting on. It isn't very practical for me to take her back to London straight away. She could hardly stay with me in the room I have now—' He came to an abrupt stop, rising slowly to his feet.

'Duncan, did Jerónimo telephone you too?' Rachel's voice rose sharply as a strong, tanned hand took a firm hold on her arm, jerking her to her feet. '*Jerónimo!*'

The Spaniard seemed enormous as he towered over her. 'Where is Paca?' he asked her.

'She wouldn't come!' Rachel wriggled her arm and his hold on her tightened, bruising her flesh. 'I only came to tell Duncan—'

'Go and wait in the car!' he cut her off. 'At once, Raquel! Señor Sutherland will excuse you.' He waited to see her go, but Rachel had no intention of going anywhere. She stood, rooted to the spot, and rubbed her arm where he had grasped her. 'Well?' he said at last.

'I don't know where the car is.'

He pointed across the road to where his car was parked illegally beside a stone wall. 'Please go now, Raquel!'

She was tempted to insist on waiting for her lemonade, but the glint in his eyes prevented her. She crossed the road blindly, uncaring of the traffic that rushed past her. What right had he to order her about? And why should she care because he was angry? It wasn't the end of the world! But it felt remarkably like the end of her world. She sat bolt upright in the front passenger seat and waited for him to finish talking to Duncan. Whatever it was he had to say, Jerónimo wasn't cross with *him*. They were both laughing when they parted.

Jerónimo opened the car door and got in beside her.

There was no sign of any laughter now. 'I'll take you home,' he said.

'But I haven't finished talking to Duncan,' she declared. 'I prefer to have lunch with him!'

To her surprise, Jerónimo actually smiled at her. 'He asked us both to join him, as a matter of fact,' he said, 'but I told him you were otherwise engaged – *to me*!'

And he took off the brake and drove off without another word.

CHAPTER TEN

THE banging on her door awoke her. For a moment she couldn't think what the noise was and was petulantly annoyed at being aroused. She had had enough trouble getting off to sleep and, although she would have liked to have blamed Jerónimo for this, honesty compelled her to admit that far from being angry he had gone out of his way to be kind to her.

'You had arranged to see Duncan, hadn't you?' she had demanded suddenly as he had driven off down the hill in silence. His last remark could only have been a slip of the tongue. His English was very nearly perfect, but it was not his native language.

'Like you, I didn't care to think of him waiting for nothing,' he had answered, 'but I couldn't get there at midday. I asked him to meet me at half-past.'

Rachel had winced at the thought of her own unnecessary journey. 'You might have told me,' she had said. 'Instead of *asking* Paca to take me out!' she had added bitterly.

'I thought you had decided to trust me,' he had answered.

'But you don't trust me!' she had appealed to him. 'If you did, you would have told me!'

'I think your feelings are mixed where Duncan Sutherland is concerned,' he had observed dryly. 'As for your sister, I thought I had impressed on you that she is no longer your responsibility?'

'Yes, you had, but, Jerónimo, I've always—'

'Yes, I know,' he had said, 'but now you have me to take care of you. I would like to think that in time you will share your worries with me and leave me to deal with them for you, as your father would have done if he had still been alive.'

The idea of his taking the place of her father had been as welcome to her as a punch in the solar plexus. She had turned away from him, shaking her head. 'My father took his worries to Carmen, not the other way round,' she had managed in a small voice.

'It happens,' he had admitted. 'But we will make a pact between the two of us, Raquel, no? You will allow me to take good care of you, and I will remember to consult you more often. *Convenido?*'

'As a sop to my English blood?' she hadn't been able to resist asking him.

But he had denied that. 'English or Spanish, you would be the same woman, *querida*. A very lovely woman with a brave heart which leads you into many foolish actions, isn't it so? For reasons that seem good to you, if you know them at all, you feel you must fight anything which curbs your independence. But it's natural for a man to want to protect what he admires and for a woman to submit to his will for her in return for his loving care. So why, I ask myself, do you have such little confidence in the powers of your womanhood that you try to usurp the man's role between us whenever I come close to you? Do you know why?'

'I was brought up to stand on my own feet,' Rachel had told him, shying away from the interested look he had given her.

'And to break your promises when it suits you? And to evade the truth whenever you find it convenient to do so?'

She had stirred uncomfortably. 'No,' she had admitted.

His flash of anger had died away. 'Then take care what weapons you use in this battle of your own making, Raquel. I may not always be as indulgent as I am being today. It's time you put away your foolish fears and faced your destiny as someone who needs to be loved and cherished, but *not* to lead some man by the nose!' He drew up alongside the house and turned towards her, patting her lightly on the cheek. 'Between us, it is I who will lead, and you who will follow, no?'

She had opened the door of the car and had stepped out. 'I won't be told what to do by you! Not as far as Rosita is concerned!' She had looked at him then and the knowledge that he was daring to laugh at her almost overcame her resolution. 'Jerónimo, it isn't that I don't trust you, but you must see that Rosita's happiness means a great deal to me and – and she confides in me!'

'That is why I have agreed to consult you. But make up your mind to it, *hija*, the final decisions concerning both Rosita and yourself will be mine. It is an amusing game that you play, but your happiness is too big a thing for me to allow you to beat me over the head with it indefinitely. You will go my way in the end!'

She had stood and watched him drive away. The look in his eyes had robbed her of her desire to attack his arrogance in retaliation for the demolition job he had done on her pride. More, she had been hard put to it not to welcome the intimacy of that glance and to stop herself from running after him, to tell him that it was not a father she wanted, not a Spanish husband, nor anyone else but him! But how could she do any such thing when it was quite plain to her that he saw her as a cousin of sorts, and sometimes as a female challenge to his masculinity, but never as a possible wife? It wasn't fair when his *machismo* rejoiced her heart and tempted her into longings where he was concerned that had never come her way before and which she wasn't sure she could handle. All she knew was that the thought of anyone else sheltering in his arms and giving him a small particle of what she could give him was an agony to her. So, she had thought, some time before she had slept, he had introduced her to the corrosive emotion of jealousy as well as everything else, and how could she possibly stay on in Spain, under the same roof as himself, when her five senses betrayed her at every turn and she touched, smelt, saw, heard, and tasted nothing that didn't increase her awareness of him?

The knocking on the door came again. Rachel turned over, her heart hammering against her ribs.

'*Quién está allí?*'

The door opened and Jerónimo snapped on the overhead light, filling the room with its dim glow. Rachel pulled the bed clothes more closely about her, blinking at him. A moment before she had been dreaming of him, but the reality of his coming was as unexpected as it was disturbing.

'What do you want?' she whispered.

He crossed the room to her bed, looking down at her with a faint smile. She had a vivid memory of how it had felt when he had kissed her and she tore her eyes away from his, afraid that he would know what she was thinking. Had he come for that? But no, it wasn't possible, not under his own roof and with herself there as his guest.

'Did you hear the telephone?' he inquired.

She shook her head and even that was an effort. What was the telephone to do with her?

'Abuela has been taken ill. She wants you to go to her.' He sat down on the edge of her bed. 'How long will it take you to get ready?'

Rachel did look at him then. 'But why me?'

'She wasn't very easy to understand, but she said something about having promised you that she would call on you.' He reached out a hand and pushed Rachel's hair away from her face. 'The Parades family, even the women, keep their word!'

'So do the Andrews!' she flared back.

He raised his eyebrows. 'So?'

'You ask too much!' she declared. 'I'm sorry I didn't leave well alone this morning, but if you'd told me, I never would have gone to see Duncan and then you wouldn't think I'd broken my word. But I *do* trust you – about some things –

and you needn't have asked Paca to take me out as if I were a child who had to be kept out of the way!'

'He stood up again. 'I do not think of you as a child, Raquel.'

'Well, you treat me as one! A child who can't possibly know what is best for it! Don't you know that people behave as they are expected to behave? It's your own fault if I find it impossible to submit to everything you say!'

'I can see you are far too cross to be resonable,' he retorted, looking amused. 'Are you always so bad-tempered when you are woken in the middle of the night?'

She gave him a severe look to hide the crumbling resolution behind her arguments. 'It depends who does the wakening!'

'And how they waken you? If I had had my way, it would not have been with a knock at your door, but like this – and this!' He stopped and kissed her first on the cheek and then on the lips, holding her close with a strength that commanded an equally fierce response from her. When he let her go, he uttered a short laugh. '*Dio mio*, you go to my head all too easily, my lovely one, but you can hardly complain that that was treating you like a child, nor did you behave like one! Perhaps I should have wakened my mother and sent her to rouse you?'

Rachel felt very small and vulnerable when he towered over her. How tall he was! She sat up, drawing her knees up to her chin, creasing the blanket with nervous fingers. It was better, she thought, to ignore his last words. 'Did Abuela say what was wrong? Is she very bad?'

'She said she would go to a doctor if you went with her.' He put a hand under her chin and forced her face up to look at him. 'How did you know she was ill? Did she tell you?'

'It was something in her face,' Rachel told him. 'I asked her what was wrong and she admitted that she had had a lot of pain that she had thought at first it was indigestion. I think it's something to do with her heart. She was very

147

frightened, though more for her maid Rafaela than for herself. I think she's all the family Rafaela has.'

'Very likely. Rafaela is older even than Abuela. It's a moot point as to who looks after whom. Will you go to her, Raquel?'

'Of course. I love her dearly!'

His face softened and he stroked her cheek. 'Yes, I think you do. She loves you too. You are very easy to love, *querida*. Too easy for my comfort!'

She put a hand up to cover his. 'How do I get to Casares?' she asked him.

'I'll drive you there as soon as you are dressed and packed. Will you be ready to start in half an hour?'

She nodded and he released her, smiling. 'That is one thing you haven't lied about,' he said over his shoulder as he walked towards the door. 'I thought I might find you with cream all over your face, but I have to believe that you use only soap and water after all!'

Rachel sat where she was for a long moment after he had gone. She didn't like his calling her a liar, nor that he thought she was liable to break her word through lack of trust in him. She longed passionately to give him her whole loyalty and to do as he suggested and to allow him to make all her decisions for her, but how could she where Rosita was concerned? Her sister had to come first, at least for a little while, even if it broke her heart not to throw her doubts and fears about Rosita's future on to his broad shoulders where he kept telling her they belonged.

She sighed, getting slowly out of bed, and began to dress in a trouser suit, the twin of which Paca had been wearing the day before. It would be a relief to go to Casares for a while, if Abuela could be prevailed upon to take care of herself and had not left it too late to agree to see a doctor. In Casares, she wouldn't have to be two people all the time, and she could dream about Jerónimo to her heart's content. She might even ask Abuela about the other girls he knew and whether he was likely to marry any of them. After all, if he had no one particular in mind— But she would not think of that now. If she didn't hurry, she would keep him waiting, and she had no wish to make him think more badly of her than he did already. She would be very cool and composed all the way to Casares, she decided, and show him that she, too, could be distant and dignified when she chose, and that she had forgotten all about his kisses and the tumult they had roused within her, a reaction he was too experienced not to have guessed at, but which she had no intention of bringing to his notice again.

Doña Nicolasa was standing in the hall when Rachel went out to the car Jerónimo had already brought round to the door.

'Will you manage by yourself, child?' she asked anxiously. 'Abuela has always been secretive about the state of her health, though less so with you, it seems! No, no, I am not offended that she should confide in you. We are all growing to rely on you, my dear, me as much as anyone, so why should I mind? I could wish Rosita had more of your ways, but I understand her less and less. To tell you the truth, I should be happy for her to go back to England if it didn't mean your going too!'

'Do you know how bad Abuela is?' Rachel countered, a little embarrassed by the older woman's praise.

'No, how could I? You must persuade her to come here as soon as she is able to travel. I've thought for a long time that it was madness for her and that old crone of a maid of hers to go on living so far away – but what will you, she is used to having her own way, that one, and only Jerónimo has any control over her.'

'Of course,' said Rachel. She saw Jerónimo in the doorway and wondered if he had heard the exchange. She hoped not.

'Raquel will manage the old lady as easily as she brings the rest of us round her thumb, Mama. You have absolutely

149

no need to worry!'

Rachel cast him a startled look, but his mother only went on fussing. 'Rachel is a young girl, not a professional nurse. You wanted her to have time to enjoy herself while she was here, not have her tied to the bedside of your grandmother. I think I should go with you!'

'No, Mama. Abuela is expecting her favourite grand-daughter to take her to the doctor and we must allow her to know best—'

'Goodness!' said Rachel.

Jerónimo's eyes met hers and she backed down hastily at the look in his. 'I see you have quite woken up!' he said smoothly.

She handed him her suitcase in silence, wishing she had held her tongue. It was a long drive to Casares and she had to school herself not to betray the singing joy in her veins whenever she was close to him, nor would it be wise to dwell on the swift kiss they had exchanged, which might have meant nothing to him, but which had confirmed her worst fears that she had tumbled so deeply in love with him that it was most unlikely that she would ever recover from the experience.

Doña Nicolasa's tiny hands clung to Rachel's as they exchanged their farewell kisses. 'Should I have wakened Rosita?' she whispered. 'Will she be cross that no one has told her where you are going?'

'She'll be crosser still if you wake her for nothing!' Rachel answered. 'If Abuela says I may, I'll telephone her this evening.'

'Very well, dear. I'll tell her, shall I? Oh, Rachel, you will make sure that Abuela does what the doctor tells her, won't you? And don't let Rafaela get in your way – she is apt to impose, you know, but Abuela has had her for so long that she would be lost without her now. Oh, and *cara*, make sure Rafaela doesn't get her hands on the medicines. She never learned to read, but she will never admit it. She wears an old pair of Abuela's *impertinentes* and pretends to read the newspaper, but spectacles or not, she can't make sense of a word of it. She'll never follow the instructions on the bottle unless you make her learn them by heart, and if you do that, she may guess that you know she can't read or write.'

'*Impertinentes?*' Rachel inquired, her eyes dancing.

'Lorgnettes,' Jerónimo supplied. 'Rafaela admired them for so long that Abuela finally gave them to her. She wears them on the end of her nose, so, holding the stick, so, and peers at one through them as if one was less than dust. It is one of her great pleasures in life.'

Rachel laughed out loud. She was constantly surprised at the indulgent way Spaniards regarded each other's eccentricities and she found she liked it very well — but then she had never felt more at home anywhere than she did in Spain.

She was still smiling when Jerónimo escorted her out to the car and held the door for her, throwing her suitcase into the back seat.

'Jerónimo, are you going to stay with Abuela too?' she asked him.

'It isn't possible. I shall have to come straight back to Granada after I have left you with Abuela. Will you find it too much for you, Raquel?'

'Of course not,' she denied. 'I thought you might be tired after driving such a long way. It's kind of you to take me.'

'I'd do this and more for Abuela,' he responded.

Of course he would! She had been a fool to think it had anything to do with her. 'I have an international driving licence,' she told him. 'I could drive myself.'

'Not in my car!' He shut the door and went round the car, getting into the driving seat with all his usual elegance. 'Why don't you try and snatch a little sleep?' he suggested. 'I'll wake you when we get close to Malaga.'

She tried to do as he suggested, but the road was too bad for her to relax sufficiently to drop off. They were building a grand new road to connect the two cities, but for the time being the old road had to suffice.

'It's a good thing your car is well sprung,' she commented after they had gone over a particularly rough patch.

'You should have travelled by road a few years back,' he retorted. 'Even this is miraculously improved.' He turned his head to glance at her through the darkness. 'You see why I didn't want you to drive yourself?'

'Oh, *yes*!' she agreed. 'Will you come and get me too, when Abuela is better?'

There was a short silence and she began to think he wasn't going to answer. 'Do you want me to?' he countered at last.

She leaned her head against the back of the seat and closed her eyes. 'Yes, I do,' she said. 'I want it very much!'

She must have slept then, for when she next opened her eyes they had joined the new part of the road that was already open, cutting through the mountains behind Malaga.

'Is Malaga as beautiful as Granada?' she asked sleepily, stretching her cramped muscles as well as she could without interfering with the gears. It had grown quite light now, though there was no sign of the sun yet. It was grey and the road was damp with dew.

'Not the bit of it we pass through.' He considered the question more seriously. 'Malaga has lost much of her previous charm recently. Torremolinos is right on her doorstep, but it is more than that. New apartments are being built everywhere and, like everywhere else in the world, they are apt to all look exactly the same. But I am prejudiced. To me, nowhere is as beautiful as Granada!'

'I think so too,' she said with satisfaction.

He had been right, she thought as they passed through the outskirts of Malaga, that part of the city held no attraction for her. The cobbles shook the car to pieces, alternating with

152

pieces of smooth tarmac here and there, and the signs that led out of the city were obscure, some of them bent and rusty and others strictly temporary as they directed the cars round the multitude of road repairs that cropped up everywhere.

It was lucky Jerónimo knew where he was going. She would have been hopelessly lost by now, especially now that the traffic was in full spate as the Malagueños made their way to work on every possible kind of machine. Rachel was glad when they had finally left the city behind, and had bypassed Torremolinos, looking down at the multitude of highrise hotels that had made what had once been a small village into one of the best known tourist resorts in the world.

The coastal road had been spoiled, in Jerónimo's opinion, but to Rachel, who had not seen it before, the scenery was still fantastic despite the density of the building schemes that were shooting up everywhere. She had not realized that Spain was such a big country. They had been travelling for hours now and, when she conjured up a map of the country in her mind, they had covered only a tiny part of one corner of it.

'Tired?' Jerónimo asked her.

She shook her head. 'I'm hungry,' she confessed.

'We'll stop in a minute and have some breakfast. Perhaps at Marbella. Can you last until we get there?'

'I can wait until we get to Abuela's if you don't want to stop,' she said, rather shyly, because she liked the idea of having breakfast on the road with Jerónimo.

'I think we can find time to feed you,' he answered.

A little while later, he pointed up into the hills and told her that the road that went up there from Fuengirola led to the little village of Mijas. 'It was once as difficult to get to as Casares, but it's now a tourist village with masses of souvenir shops.' He made a face. 'Let's hope Casares escapes the same fate!'

'You're too particular,' she teased him. 'You want to keep it all to yourself!'

153

'I want to keep Spain for the Spanish,' he admitted. 'Many small people were deprived of their land and their living to make this the play area of Europe, and the results can only be viewed with consternation by anyone who remembers what it was like before it sank under sun-tanned bodies and a pseudo-international cuisine.'

Rachel sat up suddenly, gazing back down the main street of the little town of Fuengirola. 'I remember why Mijás seems familiar!' she exclaimed. 'Lew Hoad has his tennis school there, doesn't he?'

'That's right. Do you play?'

'Not since I left school.'

'Poor little Raquel, no time for games either?'

She didn't want his pity. 'I suppose I would have made time if I had really wanted to,' she said. 'Carmen would never have stopped me from doing anything I wanted.'

They came to Marbella soon after that and Rachel admired the banks of flowers that decorated the first part of the main street. 'You seem to put in the flowers even before you've built the houses in Spain,' she said, as Jerónimo slowed and turned off into a side street to park the car.

'They're important to us,' he agreed. 'Even the poorest amongst us likes to have a nice splash of colour outside his house or apartment.' He came round the car to open her door for her. 'If you don't mind walking a hundred yards or so, we could have breakfast in the little square in the centre of old Marbella.'

She assented readily, keen to go anywhere with him, hurrying her steps to keep pace with his long-legged stride. Marbella, especially the older parts, had great charm, she thought. It was laid out in traditional Andalusian style, with narrow streets, many of them for pedestrians only, the houses with heavily grilled windows and a secret air, and dozens of pretty little corners to delight the eye. Jerónimo told her that parts of the old city wall and a section of the castle could still be seen, the castle having been built as long ago as 960 under the Caliph who ruled Southern Spain at the time to protect his territories from the menace of the Egyptian Fatimid dynasty.

'It's a pity we have no time to look at it,' he remarked, 'But, when Abuela is feeling better, she will doubtless lend you her car and you may come and explore all round here for yourself.'

Rachel didn't think she would like it half so well without him, but she murmured a gratified comment and wondered at the amused look he gave her. She sat down in the sun, brushing some imaginary dust off the leg of her trousers, and smiled back at him. 'Will you have some *churros*?' he asked her. 'Or *calenditos*?'

She looked to where he was pointing at another couple who were gulping down some crisp rings of batter, fried in huge pans of smoking hot oil. They looked good and she nodded her head eagerly. 'Yes, please,' she said.

He ordered coffee for himself and hot chocolate for her, the latter being the drink that many Spanish ladies wake up to daily, served as thick as possible so that the spoon practically stands up in the cup, yet not so sweet as much of the hot chocolate served in England. The waiter put a pile of *churros* on a piece of paper in front of her, as eager as Jerónimo to know whether they would meet with her approval. She found them delicious.

'Aren't you having any?' she asked Jerónimo, as he sat back in the sun, watching her through half-closed eyes.

'I prefer to see your pleasure in such a small treat,' he answered her. 'You are easily pleased, *niña*!'

But then it was easy to be pleased when one was enjoying oneself. She felt a moment's guilt that she should be having fun when they were on such a serious mission, but it wouldn't help Abuela if she were to put on a miserable face.

'That was lovely!' she exclaimed, wiping her fingers on the edge of the paper and draining the last of her chocolate from her cup. 'I feel ready for anything now!'

'Good.' He examined her closely. 'I thought you looked tired earlier. Don't let Abuela run you ragged.'

She shook her head. 'She won't. I didn't sleep well last night – before you came and woke me up, I mean. I'll make up for it tonight.'

'What kept you awake?' he asked immediately.

She lowered her eyelids. 'A guilty conscience,' she said lightly. 'Isn't that what always keeps one awake at night?'

'Oh?'

The single syllable made her look up quickly. 'I don't usually break my word,' she explained. 'Only I can't help worrying about Rosita.'

He looked unexpectedly pleased with himself. 'She is your first priority?' he prompted her.

'Yes. She has to be. You do see that, don't you?' she implored.

'I can see that is what you have persuaded yourself to think.' He stood up, throwing a few coins down on the table as a tip for the waiter. 'Are you ready to go?'

She got up immediately, regretting that they had to hurry on. It was warm sitting in the sun, and she could have curled up like a cat and gone to sleep with the greatest of ease.

'Is it far now?' she asked him.

'Not very far. Another hour or so,' he answered.

It seemed a long way though to her. Even when they swung off the main road and followed the narrow track that led high up into the mountains, they never seemed to get anywhere. When a lorry came the other way, they were hard put to it to pass one another without one of them going over the edge into the valley below. It was a long way down too. Then, after they had gone a few more miles, Rachel suddenly caught sight of the village below them, clinging to the sides of the mountain, one pantiled roof above another, with no way up and down that she could see, but some paths carved out of the steep side of the gorge. Jerónimo stopped the car to let her look her fill.

'That's Casares,' he told her. 'Abuela's house is some-where down there at the bottom, quite near the church.'

'But how do we get down there?' She looked, and looked again, seeing a tiny three-wheeler move down one of the narrow streets. 'Can we take the car down there?'

'But of course. Did you think you would have to walk?'

'Oh, not walk! I'd need a rope ladder at least to get up and down there!'

He laughed. 'It's not quite as steep as it looks,' he said.

He started the car again and began the slow descent, winding round the side of a cliff as the road went back on itself again and again, each time losing height until they were at last in the centre of the village, the houses crowding above them, most of them approached by a flight of steps from their neighbours in front of them. Jerónimo parked in the central square and led her to look over some railings at the far side down into the depths of the steep valley beneath them.

'You see what a shame it would be if the tourists came in their hundreds here,' he said.

'They'd never get the coaches to come down here,' she reassured him. 'The passengers would die of fright!'

'Perhaps.' He took her suitcase out of the car and led the way towards the church, pausing only to make sure she was following him. Abuela's house was only a few steps from the single street, looking exactly as Rachel had expected, with its heavily studded door standing open so that passers by could look into the beautifully tiled patio, with its masses of pot-plants and a central fountain. Jerónimo rang an ancient bell and an old woman, dressed entirely in black, came slowly towards them to let them in.

'Doña Estela is expecting you.' Tired old eyes peered into Rachel's and a faint smile touched the corrugated lips. 'She is wishing to see you, *señorita*.'

But it was Jerónimo who first caught the eye of his

grandmother as she raised her head from the pillows to greet them.

'Jerónimo, *nieto*, will you forgive me for sending for Raquel at such an hour? It was the promise I made to her, you see. Where is the dear child?'

Jerónimo hugged her very gently, kissing her wrinkled cheek. 'There is nothing to forgive, Abuelita. On the contrary, I shall be in your debt for ever. Your granddaughter had been full of the responsibility she owes to little Rosita – and see, at one word from yourself, she comes running to you, forgetting all about her sister. Now, at last, we can all see where her loyalties really lie!'

CHAPTER ELEVEN

ABUELA'S tart comment brought Rachel sharply back to earth. '*What* did you say?' she demanded.

'What you thought,' the old lady sniffed. 'Why haven't you told my grandson yet that you only came to Spain to be with him?'

Rachel was shocked. 'I never would have come if it hadn't been in Rosita's best interests,' she declared, consciously virtuous. Her eyes kindled despite herself. 'What has Jerónimo been saying?'

'You heard him yourself. Have you been interfering in his plans for Rosita? I hadn't thought you such a fool! It was obvious from the start that she would never settle down in Spain!'

Rachel moved restlessly towards the window, hiding her high colour from the old lady's eagle eye. 'There's nothing else for her to do,' she said. 'She says she wants to marry Duncan, but she can't – not just like that! She's very young and she probably doesn't know what she wants.'

'And you have taken it upon yourself to tell Jerónimo all that?'

'More or less,' Rachel admitted.

Abuela smiled. 'It's a good thing he understands you so well,' she remarked. Rachel waited in silence, anxious to change the subject, but knowing Abuela well enough to know that she would say exactly what she liked. 'Is he right when he says you abandoned Rosita without a thought to come running to me?'

'I had promised to come,' Rachel reminded her.

Abuela sank back against her pillows, looking exhausted. 'And what did you promise Jerónimo?'

Rachel turned violently. 'Did he tell you that?'

Abuela waved a feeble hand. 'Nothing. Nothing that you didn't hear for yourself.'

The television in the other room blared suddenly and Rachel gave a start, wondering what on earth was happening. It was the perfect opportunity for changing the subject, though, and she had every intention of making the most of it.

'What on earth is that?' she asked.

'Rafaela likes to look at the programmes in the morning. The government puts them out to teach the older people to read and write.' Abuela yawned. 'If you are poor enough, they supply the television too, providing you agree to follow the lessons. Rafaela is too old, poor soul, to make much of them, but she likes to look at the pictures. I think she must be getting deaf, though, she turns the sound up so high.'

Rachel sat down on the chair beside the bed. 'And what are we going to do about you?' she asked softly.

'Oh, I gave myself a fright in the night, no more than that!'

'But you are going to see a doctor? Jerónimo says the Paradise always keep their word!'

'Yes, my dear, I think I must. I thought you might drive me into Algeciras this afternoon. There is an excellent heart man there, or so his advertisement in the press would lead one to believe. We must take Rafaela with us. It's seldom that she gets out and she's had a very tiring time recently, with me being so up and down as I have been since I came home.'

'A heart man?' Rachel repeated, picking out the most essential point of all this. 'But, Abuelita, surely your doctors don't advertise, do they?'

'Why not? One soon hears all about them anyway from one's friends—'

'They don't in England,' Rachel said. 'They'd be struck off if they did.'

'But we are not in England, and in Spain you must learn

to abide by our ways, no?'

'Yes, of course.' Rachel looked suspiciously at the old lady, wondering if she were laying a trap for her by getting her to agree to such a blanket proposition. 'Within reason,' she added.

Abuela looked amused. 'It doesn't do to pick and choose,' she warned. 'For instance, we wear our wedding rings on our right hand and I noticed Rosita was proclaiming to all passing Spaniards that she is married by wearing an eternity ring there. Did this friend of hers give it to her?'

Rachel was very glad that she had no rings to wear on either hand. 'I don't know,' she confessed. 'I've never really noticed it.'

'Not very observant about your charge, are you?' Abuela mocked her.

'I do my best!'

'Leave her to Jerónimo.' The old lady's eyes softened. 'He won't send you away when Rosita goes, *chiquita*. You don't have to fear that! Cling to Rosita all you like, but it won't make any difference. Her destiny lies in England; yours in Spain.'

'You forget that I'm English,' Rachel said stiffly.

'That won't stop Jerónimo making a Spanish woman out of you if he has it in mind to do so!'

The warm colour flooded Rachel's cheeks. 'He hasn't got it in mind to do so, though he did threaten to find a Spanish husband for me. I mean to choose my own partner, though, and so I shall tell him if he brings it up again!'

'Bravo!' said the old lady dryly. 'Much good may it do you!'

Rachel said nothing. She was unutterably relieved when she heard the door-bell ring and was sent to answer it.

'Rafaela won't hear it,' Abuela told her. 'It will be the postman collecting her insurance money. Will you give it to him? You'll find my handbag on the table in the hall.'

Rachel ran to do her bidding. Rafaela was sitting on the

edge of a chair in the sitting room, her face within inches of the television screen which she peered at through very ancient' lorgnettes that she held in a rough, gnarled hand. Rachel looked at her more closely, intending to tell her not to disturb herself, when she realized that the old maid was fast asleep, and her heart went out to her in sudden sympathy. Poor Rafaela, what an anxiety it must have been to have had her mistress taken ill, with the added worry of not knowing what was to become of her if anything should happen to the Señora Doña Estela Parades Seco — Abuela, or Grandmother, to her whole family.

The postman handed her a clutch of letters and took the outgoing letters from the table in the patio. He was inclined to linger over the task of selling her the necessary insurance stamp for Rafaela. He leaned against the jamb of the door, eyeing Rachel from under long, curling lashes. '*Muy guapa!*' he breathed. 'Have you come to work in this house?'

'I am Doña Estela's granddaughter,' she told him, a little amused at his disappointment.

'An angel come from heaven!' he retorted, smiting his breast with his clenched fist and breathing more heavily than ever. 'With such hair, like the Golden Fleece, is it surprising that all men, like Jason, must try to obtain it for themselves?'

'Oh, really!' said Rachel. To receive such a blatant *piropo* at her grandmother's front door was too much for her sense of the ridiculous and she had the greatest difficulty in not bursting out laughing. 'Have I given you the right money?'

'What angel ever made a mistake over anything as mundane as money?' he riposted. 'Are you staying long, *señorita*?'

'Is that any business of yours?'

He favoured her with a broad smile, shaking his head sadly. 'You mustn't be offended, *señorita*. I meant no offence. But you are *muy simpática*, no?' He kissed the back of his hand extravagantly. '*Qué simpática!*'

Rachel shut the door with decision, a smile lingering on her face. A little surprised at herself, she recognized that she had found him *simpático* too. It was something in the warm tones of his skin that reminded her of Jerónimo. Jerónimo! Was she going to see his reflection in every man she ever met in the future?

Rafaela had roused herself while Rachel had been at the door. She came into Abuela's bedroom balancing a tray with three cups of coffee on it and sat down heavily in the chair next to the bed.

'Is it arranged that we visit doctor this afternoon? It would be better if he came here to see you, *señora*. Even with Señorita Rachel's help, you will be tired out by the time we get home and we shall have another sleepless night, like the last one!'

'But I am feeling so much better, Rafaela. It's too far for him to come here to visit me when I'm not even sure that there is anything the matter with my heart.'

'She might have been eating melons,' Rachel put in, straight-faced.

'Ah, but yes!' Rafaela pounced on the suggestion with alacrity. 'It has never suited Doña Estela to eat melons late at night. But you try and prevent her. She has more tricks up her sleeve than any of them!'

'I believe you,' Rachel agreed. 'That's why I'm hoping you will come with us, Rafaela, and make her behave herself. Don Jerónimo would wish it.'

'The *señorito* said he had put the whole matter in your hands,' Rafaela nodded. 'You have experience with doctors, I expect?'

'Not very much,' Rachel said in confident tones, 'but if we drive slowly and don't allow Doña Estela to walk a single step, she may not get too tired. What do you think?'

Rafaela was delighted to have her opinion sounded out in this way. 'Yes, Don Jerónimo would agree to that. *Mire,* there is colour in her cheeks now, so she must be feeling better!'

Rachel suspected that the old lady's colour was due to nothing more healthy than acute irritation at being discussed in this way, and she smiled agreeably at her. 'Does Doña Estela always do as you tell her?' she asked Rafaela.

The maid cackled with laughter. 'Sometimes. Ah, I could tell you some stories about her in the old days—'

'Rafaela, that is enough!' Abuela cut her off. 'Señorita Raquel has enough ideas of her own. At least I knew better than to stand at the front door and exchange pleasantries with the postman! You may well blush, young lady! What if I were to tell Jerónimo about that?'

'I'm not interested in Jerónimo's opinion of me!' Rachel disclaimed.

'Doña Estela teases you,' Rafaela consoled her gently. 'She, too, would flirt with every man who came her way. Her husband was a very jealous man and easily roused. You should have heard them together! Ah, but those were days, and now we are old and no use to anyone. It is sad. I feel heavy in the heart that we are come to this.'

'Abuela is still beautiful, don't you think?' Rachel tried to ward off the old woman's tears. 'How lucky for her that she has you to gossip with about what you both did when you were young. I know what it is when nobody remembers the little things that matter to one. I remember Carmen and my father staying at a country house in England having to ride to hounds. Carmen said it was cruel and she wouldn't go because she was sorry for the poor little fox. My father was furious as he'd wanted to make a good impression on his host and he felt Carmen was letting him down. He said it was funny she never felt sorry for the poor little bull at a bullfight. They could be heard shouting at each other all over the house! But when I mentioned it to Rosita the other day, she couldn't remember it. She was too young, I suppose.'

'But it is terrible to chase after a fox on horseback!' Rafaela exclaimed, highly diverted.

Abuela's eyes snapped with amusement. 'What are you going to give us for lunch?' she asked the old woman. 'We had better eat early and leave in good time for Algeciras.' She waited while Rafaela prised herself out of her chair and collected up the coffee cups, before turning to her granddaughter. 'You have a kind heart, little one,' she said. 'Rafaela treasures her memories as she never knew her own family. And if she exaggerates now and then, what harm does she do? You exaggerate a little yourself, perhaps? Carmen was far too lazy to have a good quarrel with anyone, and I think your father too weak to make her hunt if she didn't want to?'

'Well, yes,' Rachel admitted, 'but once roused Carmen could give a terrific performance! Rosita is just like her.'

'And what about her stepdaughter?'

'Me?' Rachel laughed. 'Loud voices upset me. I don't think I ever want to shout at anyone.' Except Jerónimo. She had wanted to shout at him often enough and, if she had it in her power, she wouldn't have been above flirting with someone else merely for the joy of making him jealous. 'I'm very English in that respect,' she added coolly.

Abuela looked amused, but she said nothing. 'I think I will try to sleep for a little while before lunch. Will three o'clock be too early for you to drive to Algeciras?'

Rachel confirmed that she would be there. She made sure Abuela had everything she wanted close beside her and then wandered out into the hot sunshine to explore the village. The shops were hidden away in odd corners, but she soon came across a bar where the old men had gathered to while away the time with a glass of something and a game of draughts or some other game. They doffed their hats as she went by and inquired after her grandmother. It seemed that everyone knew exactly who she was.

The large houses were few and far between. Most of them

were small and crowded with black-clad women hanging out long lines of washing, and pausing only to shriek a warning at the children who played up and down the narrow pathways between the houses. Here and there a donkey stood, blinking patiently into the sun, loaded with anything from sacks full of vegetables to a kitchen stove.

The time went past more quickly than Rachel was aware and she had to hurry back to Abuela's house not to keep her grandmother waiting for her lunch. But, although Rafaela had hurried all she could, it was another half an hour before she began to serve the soup she had made, and longer still before she produced some re-heated prawn fritters, which she did very slowly, portion by portion, stopping to catch her breath between every action.

The car was an unfamiliar one to Rachel. She had never driven with a left-hand drive before and she was nervous that she would forget that she had to drive on the right-hand side of the road. She and Rafaela packed Abuela into the front seat, covering her knees with a great pile of rugs. Then Rafaela climbed slowly into the back, her breathing becoming more asthmatic by the moment. Rachel, after making sure that both her passengers were comfortable, set the car up the hill that led out of the village, praying that nothing would be coming the other way. The tiny Seat bounced forward almost before she was ready for it and she let out a startled gasp as they roared up the first part of the steep incline.

'Have you driven much?' Abuela asked, her eyes firmly on the road ahead.

'Only near where we lived and a little in London,' Rachel responded between clenched teeth. This was not the moment to be put off by her own lack of experience.

Abuela relaxed with a little sigh. 'I feel safe with you,' she pronounced. 'To tell the truth I was not looking forward to the drive to Algeciras, but I think it may be very pleasant. Thank God, I feel so much better!'

She did look better, Rachel was relieved to see. The blue look had left her face and, although her eyes still held a bruised quality that could have been caused by fatigue, they were no longer lifeless – the familiar twinkle had returned to their depths, as mocking of herself as of others.

The grandeur of the scenery struck Rachel anew. The road had recently been improved so that the bus could visit the village which had formerly been completely cut off. But improved was a relative term. It was still painfully narrow in places, with nothing between the edge and the steep sides of the valleys below. On the other side, the mountains towered, made golden by the sun and covered with tough bushes that seemed to grow out of the very rock itself. But even on this road that led nowhere except to the village of Casares, there were places selling refreshments, where the local men gathered pausing in their work to crack a bottle of *manzanilla* with their friends. And they worked hard these men, pitting themselves and their bare hands against nature and coming off best, despite a still chronic lack of machinery.

By the time they reached the main coast road and turned right for Algeciras, Rachel was feeling much more confident behind the wheel. It no longer seemed strange to be driving on the right and she was able to forget the differences it made for long periods together. She couldn't help being amused too by Rafaela's pleasure at being out of the house. She sat bolt upright in the back, as proud as if she were being transported in a Rolls-Royce and not in a tiny Seat, looking from left to right as though she were afraid of missing something if she relaxed her vigilance even for a moment.

The outskirts of Algeciras were confusing and needed all Rachel's concentration, but they finally arrived in the Plaza de Generalissimo Franco and were able to park the car there next door to the Europa Chapel. It was one of the prettiest squares that Rachel had yet seen in Spain. The tiles were patterned in blues, greens and orange that shone in the sunshine and were shaded by orange trees that, even in summer, scented the air with their fragrance. Abuela told her they were bitter oranges to stop the fruit being stolen, but that when they were blown down in the winter winds and rain the entire English colony would turn out with delight to purloin the oranges to make marmalade with, the famous Seville orange being unobtainable on the open market as they were needed for the export trade with the United Kingdom.

'We have ten minutes,' Abuela went on. 'Rafaela and I will visit the church while we wait. What will you do, Rachel?'

'I'll come too,' Rachel decided.

She was impressed by the gloomy calm of the interior of the church, the richly clad, doll-faced statue of the Virgin Mary, and the wide aisles where children could sit in their prams or run up and down without disturbing too many of the other worshippers. A few ladies were seated on the wooden chairs looking blankly into space. Now and then one or other of them would flick open her fan and fan herself vigorously for a few seconds, closing it with a snap. It was the only noise to be heard and Rachel could feel the silence creeping over her and soothing away her anxieties for the old lady beside her. The gift of doing nothing without the slightest feeling of guilt was a characteristic of the Spaniard that she had always envied and, for the first time, she thought that if she stayed in Spain for long enough, it would be one that would be easily acquired.

It was not far to the doctor's surgery from the church, but the contrast could not have been more complete. The waiting room was crowded with a multitude of vociferous people, some of them openly crying, clasped hands to mouth, as they rocked backwards and forwards in the grip of sorrow that was not to be borne.

'We should never have come here!' Rachel said immediately to Abuela. 'It will be hours before he'll see you.'

But Abuela was unconcerned. 'They are here to show their sympathy, not to see the doctor. Perhaps one or two people are before us, but the rest are only friends and relations of the patients, as you are with me. Find Rafaela a chair if you can, she finds it hard to stand for long.'

Happily the old lady was quite right. As an obviously pregnant woman came out of the surgery, the crowd of people surged about her, their grief forgotten and, with much chatter and laughter, about thirty people left the waiting room, having remembered their manners just in time to utter shy greetings to the newcomers and wish Abuela good luck.

Abuela and Rachel went into the surgery alone. The doctor, a military coat hanging loose over his shoulders, was plainly horrified to see the Doña Estela Parades Seco in his surgery. 'My dear Señora, you should be in your bed, not gallivanting round the countryside like this. Why didn't you send for me in the night? You must have known I would come at once. You are not intending to come to me as a free patient? Or on the national insurance scheme? Then why take these impossible risks when they are totally unnecessary?'

Abuela had the grace to look ashamed. 'It is my maid,' she explained. 'She worries so and I thought it would reassure her if I was well enough to make the journey to Algeciras. Besides, she has spent too many sleepless nights recently and deserved to be given some kind of a treat.'

'Then you must think of some other way to bolster up her confidence,' the doctor told her gently.

He was very thorough in his examination, leaving nothing to chance, and he obviously realized how nervous his patient was of being ill, for he laughed and joked with her, making it all seem to be of no consequence, until he had cajoled the whole history of the pains she had had in her chest and the increasing, deadly exhaustion that had her in its grip.

'Well, *señora*,' he said at last, 'it is nothing very terrible after all. You have a weakness of the heart that we can control with your co-operation. It will mean more rest than you will like, and you must pay more attention to yourself and not think you are being selfish when you would like to refuse to do something and don't like to disappoint others. We will try some tablets which will help, and some ampoules that you must break, so, under your tongue, if you feel a painful attack coming on.' He turned to Rachel, anxious to include her in his soothing remarks. 'There is no need for great concern, but it would be better if your grandmother did not live by herself with only an old maid to serve her.' He half-smiled. 'She will not welcome her family's interference, I'm sure, but the time has come for her to be less independent and accept more help from them. You understand?'

Rachel nodded. 'Her family in Granada are eager to have her,' she confirmed.

'But what of Rafaela?' Abuela objected, frowning.

Rachel put her hand on her shoulder. 'Rafaela must come too. She is very old, Abuela, and deserves a rest. Sebastiana and Concha will make her welcome, I'm sure. They'll vie with one another to do things for her, and you'll have to put up with her grumbles at how badly they do everything. That won't be so bad, will it?'

Abuela's fine eyes filled with tears. 'Nicolasa—'

'Doña Nicolasa is waiting to welcome you!'

'Perhaps. But it is Jerónimo's house and when he marries his wife will be mistress there. Is it fair to her to be surrounded not only by her mother-in-law, but a grandmother as well?'

Rachel felt her grandmother's searching look, although she refused to meet her eyes. 'I think she'd be fortunate indeed to have you in the house,' she said.

'That is truly how *you* would feel about it, *pequeña*?'

Rachel nodded her head. 'You must know that!' she exclaimed.

The old lady was satisfied. 'Very well, *mi nieta y mi bisnieta*, Rafaela and I will come to Granada as soon as it can be arranged.'

Rafaela was full of forebodings about the move. Hadn't she lived in Casares all her life? It was well known that old plants transplanted badly. Had the Doña Estela thought of that?

Rachel took the old woman to look at the view of Gibraltar across the bay and begged her not to make things more difficult for her beloved mistress. 'Abuela will need you more than ever now,' she added. 'She, too, will feel strange in Granada at first.'

Rafaela was touched. 'It is hard to be old. I thank God that she has you to look after her, Señorita Raquel. I am older than she and I get tired these days with all the work there is to do, and I worry about her.' She sighed deeply. 'But now I will worry no longer. With you and Don Jerónimo to look after us we would be ungrateful indeed not to be happy in Granada.'

The drive seemed shorter on the way home. In no time they had skirted the Bay of Algeciras and had passed the comparatively modern town of San Roque, built to house the refugees from Gibraltar when the Rock became British territory in 1704, and still calling itself 'Gibraltar in Exile' as an alternative title. From there to Casares they had the road almost to themselves, managing to avoid both lorries and buses on the narrow last few miles into the village. Rachel helped her passengers out of the car and unlocked the *cancela* with the heavy key that Abuela handed her, so that they could pass in front of her into the patio.

'The telephone, it is ringing!' Rafaela announced, making no move to go and answer it. 'There must be a mistake, for everyone knows that we are in Algeciras this afternoon.'

Abuela's natural instinct was to hurry forward to answer it, but the effort was too much for her and she gestured to Rachel to do it for her. Rachel picked up the old-fashioned ear-piece and said, '*Olà, olà*' into the mouthpiece.

'Oh, Rachel, thank God it's you!' Doña Nicolasa's voice came over the wire. 'Oh, Rachel, I don't know what we are going to do. You must come home at once.' She recovered herself with difficulty. 'How is Abuela? Of course you mustn't leave her if she's not well – Is she very bad?'

'Not too bad. we've just got back from seeing the doctor—'

'She's not in bed, then?'

'No, but she ought to be. She has angina and she is going to have to be very careful and rest a great deal.'

'She must come here! Haven't I said so all along? Jerónimo will arrange everything when he comes back.'

'Comes back?' Rachel repeated. 'Where has he gone?'

Doña Nicolasa's voice became indistinct and heavy with tears. 'That's just it, nobody knows! And Rosita has gone too. Sebastiana says she saw Jerónimo go out in the car, but she couldn't see if Rosita was with him or not. I thought he was in his room having a *siesta* after his long drive—'

'*Rosita has gone?* But she must have said something to someone. Did she go out to see Duncan?'

'My dear, how should I know? I know she's your sister and that you will make every excuse for her, but she had behaved very badly ever since she got here. She pays no attention to anything I say to her – and now this! I just hope Jerónimo knows where she is and what she is doing! Rachel, I shall go mad if I don't hear from one or other of them soon.'

'Yes, it's too bad of them,' Rachel agreed. 'Jerónimo, at least, could have told you what he was up to!'

'No, no, I'm not worried about *him*. But supposing he doesn't know Rosita has gone? He will blame me for not looking after her better, I know he will! Rachel dear, I know this is asking a lot of you, but if Abuela can spare you, you must come home and find Rosita for me. You will, won't you?'

'I don't know,' Rachel said with difficulty.

'But you must! Supposing something has happened to her? No one has seen her since last night. She had no breakfast, but Sebastiana thought nothing of it because her actions are always uncertain. She might have been gone for hours! Put Abuela on, if her health is worrying you, and I'll find out how she feels about your leaving her. I need you, Rachel! They may have run off together and, although I thought Rosita would be ideal for Jerónimo, he would be bored with her in a week and she hates living in Spain.'

Rachel found she had been standing on her toes into the mouthpiece and rocked back on to her heels. 'Do you think they may have gone to look at Rosita's hacienda?' she suggested hopefully, not really believing it herself.

'No, absolutely not! I heard Rosita refuse to go anywhere near the place with my own ears. She is more than content for Jerónimo to have all the work of running the place for as long as she lives. Please come home, Rachel?'

Rachel passed the ear-piece on the end of its wire to Abuela, who had come to stand beside her. 'I won't go,' she whispered to her. 'She's Jerónimo's responsibility, but oh, Abuela, what do you think can have happened to her?'

Abuela spoke in such rapid Spanish to her daughter-in-law that Rachel lost the thread of what she was saying. This time, she vowed, she would not be found lacking in trust. This time she would wait for Jerónimo to summon her, and leave it to him to cope with Rosita's latest escapade. This time –

Abuela replaced the receiver on the wall and put her arms about Rachel in a comforting gesture. 'Nicolasa's need for you is greater than mine, Raquelita. You must go to her and keep her calm until Jerónimo gets in touch with her—'

Rachel's mouth trembled. 'Do you think something has happened to Rosita?'

'Nothing that Jerónimo isn't prepared for. You can trust

him to look after your sister, but only you can look after Nicolasa. Now, we won't cry and make ourselves miserable over nothing. It is clear that Jerónimo has everything well in hand, but Nicolasa has always been nervous when she is on her own.'

'But what about you?' Rachel cried out.

'Why, I shall busy myself packing my things to be ready for when Jerónimo comes for me. I have my tablets, Rafaela, and my faith in God, but Nicolasa has nothing to sustain her. You had best take the car and drive as far as you can before it gets dark. You're not afraid to go all that way alone, are you? If you are, perhaps you should wait until tomorrow. It is as you like, but—' she shrugged her shoulders – 'Nicolasa won't sleep a wink if she is in that house all by herself.'

Rachel returned the old lady's embrace, her heart heavy within her. 'If you think I should, then I'll go,' she said.

CHAPTER TWELVE

RACHEL turned off into the road that led to Jerónimo's house with an ineffable sense of relief. She felt glued to her seat behind the wheel and she had never been more tired in her life. The long drive in such a small car had been far more exhausting than travelling in Jerónimo's large, well-sprung saloon, even without the complications of getting lost in the outskirts of Malaga and ploughing her way through the turmoil the new road was creating, having to cross and recross through the viaducts that ran under the raised foundations of the half-built highway. After the smooth velvet surface of new link road that cut through the mountains behind Malaga, she had bounced from one pothole to the next, and already weary after her practically sleepless night of the evening before, she felt sandy-eyed and quite light-headed.

It was a few minutes after midnight when she eased herself out of the car and grabbed her suitcase from the back seat. She walked, stiff-legged, up to the front door and rang the bell, leaning against the carved stone pillar that was one of a pair supporting the roof of the porch. It opened almost immediately and Rachel was encompassed in Doña Nicolasa's soft, perfumed embrace.

'My dear child, you must be exhausted! I should never have asked it of you to come tonight – and it was all unnecessary in the end, because Jerónimo telephoned almost immediately after I had finished talking to you. *He's in England!*'

'Jerónimo is?' Rachel's voice rose to a crescendo. 'Why?'

'He followed Rosita there.' Doña Nicolasa sounded positively casual by comparison. 'Come inside, *hija*, and I'll get you something to drink. Sebastiana will have gone to bed, but I expect we can find something for you to eat too if you're hungry?'

Rachel thanked her, swaying as she stood. 'But I don't understand, Doña Nicolasa—'

'No, no, you mustn't be so formal, *cara*. We shall have to think of a new name for you to call me by, what do you think?'

'I'm too tired to think about anything at the moment,' Rachel confessed.

'Well, there's no hurry. I should have listened to Abuela when you first came here. I had thought that if you were going to call her anything as familiar as grandmother, you should have addressed her as *bisabuela*, as she was Carmen's grandmother rather than yours, but she insisted that it would all come right in the end. I shall ask Jerónimo what he thinks. Perhaps he will consent to Madre since you called Carmen by her Christian name.'

Rachel wondered what on earth she was talking about. 'Doña Nicolasa, *please* tell me what Jerónimo and Rosita are doing in England?'

But Jerónimo's mother refused to be hurried. 'Did you say you were hungry?' she asked, putting an arm round Rachel and hurrying her towards the kitchen. 'At least you must have a hot cup of something to help you sleep.'

Rachel, who was having the greatest difficulty in keeping awake, attempted a rather feeble smile. 'Does he want me to go to England too?'

Doña Nicolasa cast her a shocked look. 'Certainly not!' She slapped a saucepan on to the lighted flame and looked about her for some milk. Rachel got it out of the refrigerator and handed it to her in silence. 'Just because Rosita is a minx, I will not have you gadding about the world for the doubtful pleasure of seeing her married—'

'*Married?* To Duncan?'

'There is no need to repeat everything I say, Rachel. Even

Rosita could hardly be marrying anyone else, having slipped out of the house in the middle of the night and insisted that he take her to England with him! I was never so put out by anything! Though Jerónimo said he'd expected her to do something like that all along.'

'Did he?' said Rachel. 'If that isn't like him, when he *promised* me he'd consult me over anything to do with Rosita. And he says I break my promises!' Her eyes gleamed with tears of temper. 'Oh, just wait until I see him again!'

Doña Nicolasa looked at her anxiously. 'Now, now, dear, it wouldn't do to do anything you may regret. How could Jerónimo talk to you about what should be done when you were in Casares with Abuela and Rosita was already in an aeroplane with that Duncan of hers?'

But Rachel refused to be mollified. 'What else did he say?' she asked.

Doña Nicolasa slopped the hot milk into two mugs and looked round for the chocolate powder. 'He wasn't in a very good temper,' she said carefully. 'He was angry with me for disturbing you, and crosser still when he heard you were driving back by yourself. He wouldn't allow me to tell him that Abuela can manage splendidly without you. He said you were to go straight to bed and not be worried about anything until after lunch tomorrow.'

'Typical!' Rachel exclaimed, burning her lips on a mouthful of hot chocolate. 'And how am I expected to get a wink of sleep, worrying myself to death over Rosita, I'd like to know?'

'Jerónimo is looking after Rosita.'

'Is that supposed to console me? Well, I want to see my own sister wed – when she's old enough to know her own mind. *Duncan Sutherland* – I ask you! What is Jerónimo thinking of to allow it? What about the property she inherited from Carmen? Haven't any of them had enough sense to think about that?'

'But, Rachel, Jerónimo will go on administering it for

her as he did for her mother, and *nothing* would have made Rosita stay on in Spain if Duncan was going to be in England. She is very young, I know, but that may be why she has chosen an older man to look after her—'

Rachel choked. 'Duncan?'

Even Doña Nicolasa began to laugh. 'There must be more to him than we know,' she conceded. 'You used to like him yourself, didn't you?'

'As a friend,' Rachel agreed. It seemed strange to her now that she had ever thought of Duncan in a romantic context at all, it had been so long since she had been unable to see any other man for Jerónimo's tall, imposing frame getting in the way.

'Jerónimo will make it all respectable,' Doña Nicolasa did her best to reassure Rachel. She sighed dramatically. 'And me, I can't be entirely sorry that Rosita has left us. We shall be so much more comfortable without her, and you will have nothing to quarrel with Jerónimo about and he will like that very much and be kind to you, no? But my poor child, you are falling asleep where you sit! Off to bed with you, *hija*. We can discuss it all tomorrow when you are yourself again and when you are more accustomed to Rosita's going. Jerónimo will arrange everything so there's nothing for us to worry about. We shall enjoy ourselves and wait for him to come home to us and then he can tell us all about it.' With which comfortable reflection, she clicked her tongue at the chaos she had created in the kitchen, pulled her negligée more closely about her shoulders and wafted her way off to bed, leaving Rachel to turn out the lights behind her, and to fall into her own bed as fast as she decently could.

When Rachel awoke, Paca was sitting on the end of her bed, flicking her way through a fashion magazine. 'At last! You are awake!' the Spanish girl exclaimed. 'I thought you were never going to wake up!' She turned the magazine inside out and pointed at a photograph of herself, Diego, and

Jerónimo inside, giggling. 'Doesn't Diego look handsome? Jerónimo is more *garboso*, of course, but we all look very pretty, don't you think?'

Rachel restrained herself from saying that Jerónimo didn't look in the least dashing to her. It simply wasn't true. At the sight of his image on the paper her heart went into an acrobatic routine within her. 'You look lovely,' she managed to say.

Paca preened herself happily. 'I look lovelier now that I'm in the family way. Raquel, you must hurry up and have a baby yourself. You have no idea how nice it is to have Diego fussing about me and buying me lots of pretty things.'

Rachel chuckled. 'I can imagine,' she said dryly. 'Is that why you came to see me?'

'I came to see if you have forgiven me for yesterday morning,' Paca answered, looking suddenly subdued. 'I did want you to come with me, Raquel, truly I did. I would have asked you even if Jerónimo had not prompted me to do so. And now I want to make it up to you this afternoon. You will come, won't you? Fabiola and I are going to the Generalife gardens, and you must come too! We'll have a lovely gossip together and you can tell us what you were up to last night that you're still asleep at midday today!'

'Oh, that!'

'Yes, *that*. I hope Jerónimo knew where you were, or he'll be like a bear with a sore head for a week.'

Rachel grinned, her spirits rising at the thought. 'I'd love to come,' she said. 'Shall I meet you there, or what?'

Paca considered for a moment. 'Yes, that would be best,' she agreed. 'We'll meet you on the balcony overlooking the central pool at about half past four. Will that be convenient?'

'Marvellous,' Rachel agreed. 'I'm looking forward to meeting Fabiola.'

Paca rose to her feet and gathered up her scarf and handbag. 'You will wait if we are not there at four-thirty exactly?' she prompted Rachel. 'You will wait until we come?'

Rachel concluded that Fabiola ran on Spanish time and was incurably unpunctual. 'I'll take a book with me, then I won't mind how late you are,' she said.

Paca rewarded her with a gratified smile that quickly turned into one of her irrepressible giggles. 'Good, we'll see you then.' She dropped a light kiss on Rachel's cheek and vanished, shutting the door quietly behind her.

Rather to Rachel's surprise Doña Nicolasa raised no objection to her departing alone for her appointment at the Generalife. Indeed, she rubbed her hands with glee, insisting that there was no more beautiful place in all Granada.

'It lies on the slopes of the Cerro del Sol, behind and above the Alhambra, which you can see well from there. The views of the Darro valley and the Albaicín are magnificent also. When I think how often my husband and I went there to escape from the watchful eye of my aunt! It is the most beautiful spot on earth!'

Rachel was prepared to take that with a pinch of salt but, by the time she had climbed the hill and had walked under the thick trees to the entrance of the Generalife, her appetite was whetted and she felt a keen anticipation for what lay in store for her. Having bought her ticket, she wandered slowly down an avenue of cypresses, pausing to admire the oleanders that arched over the higher path on the right-hand side.

She came first to the open-air theatre that is used every June for performances of the best music and ballet. It seemed an ideal setting for such a project and she was sorry that by the following June she would probably be back in England and would never hear it for herself. The auditorium was divided by a series of low box hedges that added to the intimacy of the place. Even from here the music of running water could be heard and Rachel contented herself with that, drinking in absence of human sounds that seemed to pervade the atmosphere. How peaceful it was, and how much she longed for Jerónimo's presence that would make it all perfect for her!

She found the central pool without difficulty and sat down on one of the seats, watching the plumes of spray that fed it from the dozens of fountains on either side. It was blissful to be out of the direct rays of the sun for a while, and she could only admire whoever it was who had had the inspiration to use water as much as flowers as the first priority in planning his garden. It was not yet half past four, so Rachel took out her book and pretended to herself that she was going to read, but the volume lay slackly in her hand and, after a while, she closed her eyes and allowed the tranquillity of the garden to take possession of her, guiltily hoping that Paca and her friend Fabiola would be delayed and not disturb her too soon.

'Hullo, my darling Raquel. Are you still tired that you must sleep in the middle of such exquisite beauty?'

For a moment Rachel thought she was dreaming. She had wanted Jerónimo so badly that her mind, playing a cruel trick on her, had called up his image to taunt her with the physical longings that seized her whenever she allowed her thoughts to escape the rigid control she had determined to impose on them.

'Jerónimo,' she said weakly.

He bent forward, bringing his face level to hers, examining her features with a light in his eyes that made her melt inside. 'I should be angry with you for driving all that way by yourself,' he went on. 'What did you think you could do for Rosita in Granada that I couldn't better for her in England, niña?'

'I didn't come back because of her, but because of your mother. All she knew was that Rosita had gone without a word to anyone and she didn't know where you were either.' She managed a brief smile. 'I think she thought the pair of you had eloped!'

'But you were able to reassure her about that?'

'I didn't think it likely,' Rachel confessed.

'You knew it was impossible for me to do any such thing! It is just the sort of extravagant idea my mother would dream up because she had to have a good excuse for you to feel that you had to keep her company despite Abuela's first call on your sympathy—'

'No, no, you are too harsh, Jerónimo. Besides, it was Abuela herself who told me to come back to Granada.'

Jerónimo sat down on the seat behind her, taking possession of her hand in his. 'How is Abuela?'

'Not too bad. She insisted that I took her into Algeciras to see the doctor, though I think he would have preferred to come to her. She wanted Rafaela to have a nice outing! Rafaela is rather a dear, isn't she?'

'She ought to have been retired years since, but Abuela won't hear of it. This time, however, I shall insist that other arrangements are made for Abuela's comfort, whatever objections she makes. She is too far away in Casares. I shall speak to her about it!'

Rachel's lips curved into a triumphant smile. 'I did,' she said. 'She and Rafaela are both coming to live in your house here. I'm sorry if you don't like it, having them under your feet all the time, but the doctor said she shouldn't live on her own any longer—'

Jerónimo looked stunned. 'You persuaded Abuela to live with *us*?'

'Well, yes,' Rachel admitted. 'Do you mind very much?'

'*Mind?* Dear heart, I've been trying to persuade her to do just that for years! First she would pretend that my mother wouldn't like it, and then it was that she wouldn't like my future wife, and always there were Rafaela's feelings to be taken into consideration. How did you do it?'

'I don't know.' The colour rose in Rachel's cheeks. 'I

didn't know you were thinking of getting married. You've never mentioned your fiancée.'

'I wouldn't – to you!'

Rachel considered that, trying to hide the hurt he had dealt her. 'I hope you'll be very happy,' she said quietly.

'I intend to be, if the girl of my choice is of the same mind. She might not like to live in a house with so many other women already there – my mother, and now my grandmother—'

'I think she'd be lucky to have the chance!' Rachel burst out. 'But weren't you taking rather a risk, importing Rosita and me to live with you? You couldn't have known that it would be for such a short time.' She blinked, shattered by the thought of having to leave Spain. She had been fooling herself before, she thought, for she had had very little intention of actually packing her bags and going back to England in Rosita's wake. She had been quite sure in the back of her mind that Jerónimo would have found some way to prevent her leaving. 'How is Rosita?'

Jerónimo looked amused. 'I wondered when you were going to ask.'

'You promised you would consult me about her future,' she reminded him, her voice sharpened with pain. 'You accused me of breaking my word, but you didn't even tell me she'd gone!'

He sat back, watching her through half-closed lids. 'I thought you had your hands full with Abuela.'

'Yes, I did. But you could have told me all the same!'

'I did try, but you had already left for Algeciras. I nearly missed the plane, as a matter of fact, and had to leave phoning Mama until I got to England, but tell me the truth, Raquel, were you really worried that Rosita couldn't manage without you to hold her hand, or was it just that it's become a habit for you to look after her?'

Rachel baulked at answering that directly. 'I knew she'd be all right with you,' she compromised.

He let out his breath in an audible sound and smiled at her. 'You trusted me to see her married to that stuffed shirt Duncan, and to come hurrying back to you?'

'Yes,' she said. She moved restlessly. 'I don't know what brought you here, but I'm supposed to be meeting Paca and a friend of hers.'

He nodded. 'In the north portico of the Patio de la Acequia at half past four. Paca is a very reliable messenger. I thought you might be waiting somewhere else, or that you might lose your way, but there you were, with your lovely hair all round you—'

'Like Jason's Golden Fleece,' Rachel interrupted, a laugh gurgling in the back of her throat.

He raised an inquiring brow. 'Now where did you hear that?'

She told him about the postman at Casares. 'He was sweet!'

'You had no business to listen to him!' he frowned at her. 'Why did you?'

She could hardly tell him that it was because he had reminded her of him, so she turned the conversation back to Paca's perfidy. 'I do think she might have told me that it was you who wanted me to come here!' she exclaimed. She turned to look at him, indignation written plainly on her face. 'Why did you? You could have seen me just as well at home!'

'With Mama on hand to chaperon you,' he said wryly. 'It was not to be thought of!'

'I expect she wants to hear about Rosita as much as I do,' Rachel argued with him.

'Then she'll have to wait until this evening,' he retorted. 'I did not go to the trouble of telephoning Paca first thing this morning, and having to hang on for nearly an hour while they routed the call from pillar to post all through Europe, merely to tell you about your sister's tantrums and Duncan's sulks, while I rushed about London, getting a special licence and arranging for them to have some kind of ceremony before they settled down in that dreadful room that Duncan calls a "flat", in which there was hardly any furniture at all! To see Rosita cooing over the drizzling rain, and her naked relief to be living in that shoebox in London, and not in my beautiful home in Granada, was a salutary experience I hope never to repeat. You, my love, have an obligation to be very kind to me to make up to me for all I have suffered in the last twenty-four hours!'

She laughed. 'I'll try,' she promised.

The look in his eyes caressed her. 'You won't have to try very hard. A beautiful woman set in a beautiful garden is as much as any man can ask.'

She looked down at her feet. 'The garden is far more beautiful than I. If you seek tranquillity, look around. I'm afraid I can't compete.'

'To me you are more beautiful even than the Garden of the Architect,' he said in her ear. 'You are a delight to my eyes and have been since the first moment I saw you.'

'You shouldn't embarrass me with *piropos* when you are thinking of getting married!' she rebuked him, and then, when he was silent, she added, completely ruining her effect, 'Have I seen the Garden of the Architect?'

'This is it,' he told her. 'Didn't you know? Generalife is a corruption of *Gennat Alarif*, the Garden of the Architect.' He looked up as some other people came into the portico and pulled her to her feet. 'There are too many people here. Let's stroll through the Carmen de los Mártires where I can talk to you alone.'

She was sorry to leave the formal splendour of the little walled garden, but walking amongst the groves of trees, where once the food stores, the Moslem dungeons had been sited, and the field where tournaments and parades had once been held in medieval splendour had its own delights, particularly as Jerónimo seemed content to slow his pace to hers, holding her hand with all the unselfconsciousness of the Spanish male out with a girl.

'What did you want to say to me?' she asked him after a while. 'Did you only want to know about Abuela?'

'I want to talk about you,' he answered. 'We can't put off the decision about your future any longer—'

'I shall go back to England!'

'No, my love, you will stay in Granada. Didn't I tell you I would find a Spanish husband for you? Well, now I wish to tell you about him.'

Her throat felt so dry it hurt her to swallow. 'I don't want to hear about him! I don't want to marry anyone, certainly not at your bidding. I'm sorry to disappoint you when it would be so much more convenient if I'd allow you to dispose of me like any grateful pensioner should, but I can't!'

'Nevertheless, you will listen to me, if I have to keep you here all night, which I would like to do very much, so you had better be careful how you tempt me with your talk of how grateful pensioners should be disposed of, or I shall claim your kisses as an earnest of your debt to me—'

'Oh, Jerónimo, how can you?' Her voice broke and she pulled her hand out of his. 'How can you talk of marrying me to someone I don't even know and kissing me yourself all in one breath?'

He grasped her by the shoulders, turning her to face him, lifting her face with his fingers cupped beneath her chin. 'How stupid you are, *querida*,' he said lovingly. 'Didn't you ever think that I might be the Spanish husband I have in mind for you? Whom else should I want to marry but you?'

'Me?'

He touched his lips to hers. 'How could you not know?' he wondered.

'But, Jerónimo, you can't marry me! Think how your mother would dislike it! Even if she got used to my being English, she'd never think I was good enough for you.

Everyone would think you'd gone mad!'

'Mad with love for you! Why not? Raquel, this is not the moment to argue with me. If I cannot have your consent to marry, then I shall marry you without, and we shall see how long you hold out against me before you come willingly into my arms and admit that you are mine!'

'I'd do things all wrong and irritate you—'

'Is that all you have to say?' he demanded, pulling her closer against him. His lips met hers again, kissing her with the soft touch of a feather, but which she recognized as a token of his firm intention of commanding her response, whether she would or no. '*Bienquista*, how can you think so little of yourself? Don't you know that you are already the central pivot of my entire family? My mother preens herself and tells me you must learn to call her Madre and that I must speak to you about it at once. My grandmother comes hurrying to Granada at your bidding and won't go to the doctor without you, because only you have broken down her dislike of being fussed enough to realize she is really ill. And I – I come to England to settle the affairs of Carmen's daughter, and you break my heart with your proud ways and your insistence that you should work to support yourself – and Rosita too! I rack my brains for some way to convince you that you need me to look after you, until I can find a way of telling you of my need for you, and you argue and argue about it and say you will never be mine! But now you will argue no more, because my patience is at an end and I shall make love to you so beautifully you won't have the heart to resist me, *favorita*, and gradually you will learn to love me too!'

She listened to him, at first with astonishment, and then with a blaze of happiness that shone out of her and brought an approving gleam into his eyes.

'But Jerónimo, you are the head of the family. Even Abuela does as you tell her—'

'But you do not?'

'That's what I'm trying to tell you,' she said. 'I want only that! Please let me be the garden you want to possess as your own, to bring you peace and tranquillity if I can.' Her eyes met his bravely. 'The war of independence went badly for me, *querido*. You hurt me when you said I lacked faith in you and had lied to you, because even then I only wanted to please you, and I was torn in two between what I felt for you and what I felt I ought to do for her. How right you were when you told Abuela that my going to her had revealed my true priorities! But I had no idea before that moment that Rosita had already gone away from me, but she had. For me, there is only you!'

He put his hand to her face, intrigued as always by the soft fairness of her skin. 'If you had not wanted me, you would have denied it when I told Duncan you were engaged to me—'

'I thought it was a slip of the tongue!'

'It was as well for you I didn't show that,' he told her soberly. 'I was jealous enough of your friendship with Duncan Sutherland. As it was, I thought you were beginning to accept that I meant to have you, that I was the destiny I had prophesied for you in London.'

She turned her lips into the palm of his hand. 'I wanted it too much to allow myself to hope.' She looked up at him, a new doubt in her eyes. 'Are you sure, Jerónimo? I thought sometimes you didn't like me very much.'

'There were many times when I didn't like you at all! Often I should have liked to slap you as you once thought to slap me, but I knew it would have ended with you in my arms, like now, and you had to have time to fight and lose the battle you were putting up against me. It was too easy to make you submit before you were ready to want it as much as I did.'

She buried her face against his neck. 'Did you know all the time?' she asked him, humbled by his restraint.

'That you found me attractive, that I knew,' he argued,

'but that you loved me, that I could only hope.'

'I love you more than I can ever tell you,' she said. 'I think I loved you even in London, but I didn't know until you took me to the Alhambra and quoted that Moorish poet to me and kissed me.' She sighed deeply. 'How wonderful to think that I can stay with you for ever! I was miserable every time I thought of going away from you, but I never thought for one moment you'd marry *me*!'

Her satisfaction made him laugh. He tipped back her head and kissed her hard. 'I have another poem for you,' he murmured. He kissed her again and she clung to him. 'A poem which reminds me of you,' he went on in a thrilling, low voice, 'and which I shall quote to you often—'

'Tell me,' she said, exploring the inside of his shirt collar with her fingers for the sheer joy of touching him.

'Said Ibn Zamrak, "Granada is a bride whose crown and jewels and robes are flowers; her tunic is the Generalife ... her pendants the clusters of the morning dew".'

Rachel stood very still in the circle of his arms. 'You love Granada very much, don't you?' she said. Would he ever love her as much? she wondered.

He smiled, looking very arrogant and sure of himself, and she realized that like every Spaniard he would always be tempted to test the strength of her love by arousing her jealousy, though he would be equally quick to reassure her and far more passionate than she would ever be.

'Granada is my first love; you are my last love and the crown of them all!' he whispered to her.

It was the last sane thing that either of them was to say for a very long time to come.

Each month from Harlequin

8 NEW FULL LENGTH ROMANCE NOVELS

Listed below are the last three months' releases:

PLEASE NOTE: All Harlequin Romances from #1857 onwards are 75c. Books prior to that number, **where available** are priced at 60c through Harlequin Reader Service until December 31st, 1975.

These titles are available at your local bookseller, or through the Harlequin Reader Service, M.P.O. Box 707, Niagara Falls, N.Y. 14302; Canadian address 649 Ontario St., Stratford, Ont. N5A 6W4.

Q

Have You Missed Any of These
Harlequin Romances?

☐ 427 NURSE BROOKES
      Kate Norway
☐ 438 MASTER OF SURGERY
      Alex Stuart
☐ 446 TO PLEASE THE DOCTOR
      Marjorie Moore
☐ 458 NEXT PATIENT, DOCTOR
      ANNE, Elizabeth Gilzean
☐ 468 SURGEON OF DISTINCTION
      Mary Burchell
☐ 469 MAGGY, Sara Seale
☐ 486 NURSE CARIL'S NEW POST
      Caroline Trench
☐ 487 THE HAPPY ENTERPRISE
      Eleanor Farnes
☐ 491 NURSE TENNANT
      Elizabeth Hoy
☐ 494 LOVE IS MY REASON
      Mary Burchell
☐ 495 NURSE WITH A DREAM
      Norrey Ford
☐ 503 NURSE IN CHARGE
      Elizabeth Gilzean
☐ 504 PETER RAYNAL, SURGEON
      Marjorie Moore

☐ 584 VILLAGE HOSPITAL
      Margaret Malcolm
☐ 599 RUN AWAY FROM LOVE
      Jean S. Macleod
      (Original Harlequin title
      "Nurse Companion")
☐ 631 DOCTOR'S HOUSE
      Dorothy Rivers
☐ 647 JUNGLE HOSPITAL
      Juliet Shore
☐ 672 GREGOR LOTHIAN, SURGEON
      Joan Blair
☐ 683 DESIRE FOR THE STAR
      Averill Ives
      (Original Harlequin title
      "Doctor's Desire")
☐ 744 VERENA FAYRE, PROBA-
      TIONER, Valerie K. Nelson
☐ 745 TENDER NURSE, Hilda Nickson
☐ 757 THE PALM-THATCHED
      HOSPITAL, Juliet Shore
☐ 758 HELPING DOCTOR MEDWAY
      Jan Haye
☐ 764 NURSE ANN WOOD
      Valerie K. Nelson

PLEASE NOTE: All Harlequin Romances from #1857 onwards are 75c. Books prior to that number, **where available** are priced at 60c through Harlequin Reader Service until December 31st, 1975.

TO: HARLEQUIN READER SERVICE, Dept. N 509
    M.P.O. Box 707, Niagara Falls, N.Y. 14302
    Canadian address: Stratford, Ont., Can. N5A 6W4

☐ Please send me the free Harlequin Romance Catalogue.
☐ Please send me the titles checked.

    I enclose $_____ (No C.O.D.s). All books listed are 60c each. To help defray postage and handling cost, please add 25c.

Name _____

Address _____

City/Town _____

State/Prov. _____ Postal Code _____

AAA-1

Have You Missed Any of These
Harlequin Romances?

PLEASE NOTE: All Harlequin Romances from #1857 onwards are 75c. Books prior to that number, **where available** are priced at 60c through Harlequin Reader Service until December 31st, 1975.